Chapter I

Cash Lopez

What was supposed to be the happiest day of my life turned out to be the worst. I was supposed to be happily married and celebrating the day of my Abuelita's birthday. I was torn between wanting to find the muthafuckas that shot up my wedding, killed my friend, and not to mention, I'm ready to put a bullet in my supposed to be husband.

She's Pregnant! Replayed over and over in my mind with the vision of that hoe Tiffany being rolled out on a stretcher. To say I was beyond ecstatic would be an understatement. I was ready to commit a crime, making Brooklyn my victim.

My heart hurt, my blood was boiling and as bad as I wanted to scream, I held it in.

"Cash!" my mother shouted, knocking me out of my thoughts. She had been calling my name, but I was in my own world.

1

Barbie Scott
TRAP GYRL 3

"Sorry, Mommy. Yes?"

I looked at her with sympathetic eyes. The look plastered on her face made me stress even more. I couldn't even help myself, the tears began to pour rapidly; I was a wreck. I had so much to cry over and the part I hated most was, I knew I was stressing my baby out and I couldn't help it. I clutched my big round belly and said a silent prayer, something I'd been doing a lot lately.

For me, for Niya, and for the innocent people that came to support us but didn't make it out alive.

Before I could say Amen, my father began shouting at the top of his lungs, causing me and my mother to turn around in our seats. Even the limo driver jumped at the roar of his voice.

"You bring me that fucking Mario's head on a platter, Saul! I don't give a fuck how you do it, just do it and if you don't...You're a dead man!" he hung up the phone.

The look in his eyes sent a chill throughout my body. Never in my life had I ever heard Esco raise his voice or even declare war. Esco was a true Boss but a killer, he wasn't. He believed in helping people. He took care of needy families and the only thing would make him catch a body was someone playing with his money. But, he had people that would get the job done for him. When he got shot at the wedding, I nearly lost it. Thank God, he was smart enough to wear his bulletproof vest to the wedding.

The sound of my mother's ringing phone caused the entire car to stop, knowing it could be more bad news, I prepared myself for the worst.

"Habla, mi?" my mother answered, in Spanish. "Oh, nooo!" she shouted. Tears instantly fell from her eyes, which was weird because my mother never cried.

We couldn't hear what the caller was saying but the look on her face told it all.

"I'm on my way," she spoke sadly then disconnected the line. "Miami Memorial," she told the driver and he made an illegal U-Turn quickly.

"Ma, what's wrong?"

"Que was shot," she cried, hysterically.

"Oh my God." I held my chest in disbelief.

That's why he didn't show up to the wedding, I thought to myself as the tears began to fall.

I looked at my mother and her hands were shaking as she dialed on her cell phone. I said another silent prayer, now for Que, and shook my head repeatedly.

Barbie Scott
TRAP GYRL 3

"Blaze, meet me at Miami Memorial. Que was shot," she spoke into the phone, and then quickly hung up.

Shit was getting weirder and weirder by the day. Que was shot, Niya was dead, and this bitch Tiffany was shot and pregnant by my husband. I don't think I could deal with any more bad news.

When we pulled up to the hospital, I wobbled in, followed by my mother and father. We stopped at the receptionist desk and they informed us Que was on the 5th floor in surgery. When we made it upstairs, we headed to the second receptionist desk. The nurse told us that a doctor would be out shortly to speak with us. We took a seat in the waiting area and waited patiently, all we could do was hope for the best.

"Family for Quintin Johnson?" the doctor called out.

We jumped to our feet and rushed over to him. He looked me up and down, observing all the blood on my dress. I shook my head, ensuring him that it was a long story. He looked away then began speaking.

"Mr. Johnson was shot several times. He had a bullet plunged into his shoulder that we couldn't remove. Another bullet hit him in the chest and

TRAP GYRL 3

caused one of his lungs to collapse. He also took two bullets to the abdomen. One went through this abdomen and came out, and the other bullet was surgically removed. For the most part, he is doing great but the young lady that was with him was seriously wounded and is in an induced coma."

Young lady? I thought to myself and it all began to make sense.

"Breelah!" I shouted right when Brooklyn and Blaze rushed through the doors.

Me and Brooklyn immediately locked eyes and if looks could kill, he'd be dead right where he stood. He dropped his head in shame. He looked so broken that I wanted to run into his arms but NOPE! not going to happen.

He walked over to the doctor and asked about Bree. After the doctor informed him of her condition, he walked over to take a seat. The moment his tears fell, I broke down, instantly, behind him. It had been so long since I saw my husband cry and that shit was breaking me.

Brooklyn Nino

Everything just seemed to be falling apart in a matter of one fucking day. Looking at my wife in a bloody wedding gown broke a nigga down even more. My little sister was shot, Carter was missing in action, and I had let Cash down with this whole Tiffany situation. I didn't have anybody to turn to. I don't have any family, but Cash and her team, so a nigga had to pretty much mourn alone. I knew I fucked up this time but right now was the time I needed Cash most. I was just too ashamed to talk to her.

Lord, heavenly father, please let my little sister be ok. Please heal her wounds, Father God. Please don't take the only thing I have, Lord. I don't give a fuck, I'll leave the game. (excuse my language but I'm so serious.) My sister has a future ahead of her so if you hear me, I beg you to please spare her life. Amen. With my head buried into the palm of my hands, I couldn't do shit but pray. I wasn't much of a spiritual person but this was the time I needed to believe that the lord was indeed a savior. I just hoped he heard my cry for help.

Barbie Scott
TRAP GYRL 3

"You good, my nigga?" Blaze asked, taking a seat beside me.

"Really, nah, Blaze. I can't lose her, man. She's all a nigga got out here. Besides Carter and Cash, and clearly, Cash ain't fucking with me, I ain't got nobody."

"Just have faith, Nino. Bree gone pull through," he said and rubbed my back.

"I fucked up, man," I said and faced him. "The fucking EMT shouted out that Tiffany was pregnant when they were rolling her out the chapel on the stretcher."

"What?" Blaze shouted with his eyes bulging.

"Hell yeah. I didn't even know she was pregnant until she texted me right before the wedding had started. I haven't seen that girl in months so she gotta be at least four or five months." I shook my head.

"So, how she's doing?"

"Shit, I don't know, but she's in here somewhere."

"Well, you gotta check on her, man. I know Cash will die, but shit, you gotta check on yo seed."

"I know," I replied, quickly, leaving that conversation alone.

Barbie Scott
TRAP GYRL 3

Nina, Carlos, and Diane walked in and ran to Cash's side. She was crying hysterically as they all hugged each other in a group. Ms. Lopez was rubbing her back as Esco paced up and down the hall on the phone. The look in his eyes told me that he was ready for war. As bad as Ms. Lopez was trying to keep her cool, she as well looked as if she were ready to call in the troops.

Shit was about to get hectic in these streets and I was ready. I needed the muthafuckas who shot my sister and every last muthafucka who shot up my wedding. I've called my brother over and over, not once getting an answer. That shit was making me furious than I was already. Here his little sister was laying up in the hospital, nearly dead, and this nigga was nowhere to be found...

***

After hours of waiting for Bree to be sent to a room, they finally came and told me I could go visit her. Everyone had finally gone up to see Que so I had to do this alone. I walked into her room and the moment I saw her, my eyes flooded my face with tears. She was connected to so many wires and machines. Her head was swollen almost where you couldn't recognize her. She laid there peacefully in a coma so I decided to talk to her. I just prayed she could hear me.

"I love you, little sis. I hope you could hear me. I need you to pull through because, without you, I have no one. I'm so sorry this happened to you, Bree."

I dropped my head and tears rolled onto the floor. The only sound you could hear throughout the room was the sound of her heart monitor. I kept talking to her until I had dozed off in the chair next to her bed.

When I opened my eyes, it felt as if I had slept for hours. I looked over at the TV tray beside her bed, and there was a flower pot with flowers, balloons, and a teddy bear attached to it. I lifted out my seat to retrieve the card.

My dearest Bree,

Girl, you've turned me holy. I don't think I've prayed this much in my entire life. Lol. I pray you pull through this but I know you're a soldier so I know you will. I love you, lil sis. I'll be back to see you soon.

Cash.

Barbie Scott
TRAP GYRL 3

I couldn't help but smile at the card. What's crazy is, I never heard her walk into the room.

I must have really been tired.

I bent over and placed a soft kiss on Bree's forehead then made my way out the door. I walked to the nurse's station and gave them Tiffany's name. The nurse informed me she was doing well, the baby was ok, and she was in room 533. I walked over to the room and braced myself before entering.

When I walked in, she was also connected to machines but facing the window. I guess she was fully awake because she quickly looked over at me. We both just stared at each other not saying one word. I mean, shit, I really didn't know what to say. She instantly began to cry. I walked near her bed to comfort her.

"How are you feelin', ma?"

"Like shit," she cried. "I'm so sorry, Nino."

"You good, Tiff."

"I know you're upset with me and I really want to apologize. But just put yourself in my shoes. I really love you."

"Just tell me this, ma. Why did you come to the chapel, though?" I asked, and she dropped her head. She looked so ashamed, therefore, she cried harder.

Barbie Scott
TRAP GYRL 3

"Honestly, I figured if I objected to the marriage, you wouldn't do it. I really love you and I didn't want you to Marry her," Tiffany said, truthfully.

"But, Tiff, that wasn't a good idea, ma. You know I love Cash, and nothing is going to change that. I'm sorry you felt I led you on, but I just got caught up."

"So, there's never going to be an us?" she asked with pitiful eyes.

I didn't know what to say so I just shook my head no.

"How many months are you?" I asked, looking at her stomach. It was small and round but she was, in fact, pregnant.

"Almost five months."

The moment she said five months, I began shaking my head because I knew it was too late for her to get an abortion. Right then, I knew that it was the end of me and Cash. She would never want me back knowing I bared a child with another woman.

"Look, ma. I'ma be here for my seed but me and you will never be together. Right now, my wife is upset at me because she heard the EMT say you were pregnant. I'm going to do everything in my power to get her back so, Tiff, please don't cause

any more havoc in my marriage. Like I said, I'ma
be there for my baby but me and you will never be."
I used my finger to point from me to her.

She turned her head to look out the window, so
I took that as my cue to leave.

I walked out of her room so stressed out, I
needed to go home and get some rest. The moment I
made it into the hallway, Cash and I locked eyes.

Shit! I cursed myself because she had caught
me coming out of Tiffany's room.

The look she gave me let me know that she was
hurt. She shook her head and stormed off towards
the elevator.

I mean, what did she expect? The girl was laid
up shot and not to mention, with my baby. I hopped
on the elevator to the first floor and exited the
hospital. I jumped in my whip and headed home.

Chapter II

Cash Lopez

<u>*One Month Later...*</u>

Today is one of the worst of the many days of my life. I couldn't believe that I was about to bury one of my friends. After a whole month of investigation, they had finally released her body to the funeral home so today was the day to say goodbye.

Deep inside, I knew they wouldn't solve the case and especially because I paid top dollars to have the security system in the church deactivated right before the wedding. In all honesty, I didn't need the police handling anything because I was gonna handle everything on my own; pregnant or not.

Over the last few weeks, the streets had been pretty quiet but that wouldn't be for long. All I wanted to do was bury my friend then the entire city of Miami would feel my pain. Christmas passed, New Years passed, and so much was going on with my crew that we didn't celebrate any holidays. How could we celebrate? Bree was laid up half dead, Que was shot, Niya was dead, and I wasn't fucking with my husband right now.

Fuck a Holiday!

I had been in contact with Niya's family over the past month. I gave them the money to cover the entire funeral service, it was the least I could do. Niya's dress and her casket were baby pink because it was her favorite color. We would be releasing twenty-two doves and she also had a horse and carriage. Looking in the mirror, I couldn't help but reminisce on all the times we had. The good, the bad, and the ugly. Regardless, she was still my dear friend. Apart of me felt as if it was all my fault. Knowing the beef we had with the Cartel, I should have kept my wedding private. But, I failed my friends and I was paying for it.

Que was up talking but he was pretty fucked up. Bree was still in a coma and Carter was still missing in action. I haven't said much to Brook, and I planned to keep it that way. I knew I was being selfish about the situation with him and Tiffany because, of course, the baby could have been conceived during their two-month fling but I was hurt at the fact of him almost letting me walk down that aisle without telling me. He knew she was pregnant so he should have at least gave me a choice. How could I be with him knowing he shared something so special with another woman? I loved Brook to death but moving on was something I had to do. I was already hurt knowing Tiffany had a piece of the man I loved the most, but a baby? A fucking baby? Nah, I can't do it.

"Cash, let's go, Mija." My mother entered my room, knocking me out my thoughts.

I grabbed my clutch and headed down the stairs. I stopped at the kitchen and grabbed a croissant from the deli tray because I didn't want to starve my baby any longer. Lately, I'd been having mild stomach aches, I knew it was due to all the stress, which was something I hated. My gut feeling was telling me I wouldn't make it through the entire nine months, but I was gonna try.

I walked outside and my mother and Esco stood by the limo waiting for me. I took a deep breath before we pulled off and tried my hardest to hold up.

Barbie Scott
TRAP GYRL 3

***

Though I'm missing you
(although I'm missing you)
I'll find a way to get through
(I'll find a way to get through)
Living without you
Cause you were my sister, my strength, and my
pride
Only God may know why,
Still, I will get by

The moment the song came on, I broke down. As bad as I tried to hold it in, I couldn't. I couldn't call my friend, see my friend, or even laugh with my friend anymore. Our last encounter was the day in the mall when Nina went into labor. The memory made me smile to myself just picturing Niya's face. She looked so nervous. I dropped my head and cried so hard that my baby began to do somersaults in my belly. Suddenly, I felt a hand on my shoulder. When I looked up, Brook stood there with a look that almost broke me down more.

Saved by the bell, I thought to myself because the usher walked up to inform us that it was now time to view the body.

Barbie Scott
TRAP GYRL 3

I stood up, excusing myself from Brook, and walked over to the casket.

"It's all your fault, bitch!" Niya's mother, Nathine, shouted through tears.

I stood there frozen, not knowing what to say. She was shouting all types of obscene words that cut deep.

"It's your fault. You dope dealing, thug bitch!" she continued to shout.

She ran up in my face and all I could do was block her shot. I used my arms to cover my face and when I looked up, Ms. Nathine was on the floor. My mother was standing over her, now shouting.

"You could say what you want to Cash, but you putting your hands on her ain't happening, bitch. I'll make your life a living hell," my mother told her in an aggressive tone.

I grabbed my mother's arm to pull her away but she wasn't budging. Brooklyn and Blaze ran over and grabbed her, pulling her out of the church. I shot Ms. Nathine one last look before walking out the service.

Looking out of the limo's window, all I could do was cry. Ms. Nathine was right. It was my fault and I beat myself up over and over about the entire situation. What was crazy was she was fine the

entire time I had met with them, so I assumed
seeing her child lying in a casket was unbearable.

"Ouch!" A sharp pain hit me, making me clutch
my stomach.

"Cash, are you ok?" my mother asked. "Yeah,
ma, I'm fine." I looked over at her.

"Mija, please don't stress my grand baby out.
It's not your fault."

"I'm sorry, ma. But it is my fault. I knew things
could get ugly and I still chose to have my wedding
publicly."

"No, my child. It's not your fault. Nobody
knew they were coming to shoot the wedding up.
We were at a church, for God sake," she said then
looked out the window, falling into a daze.

"Valentino, go to the warehouse," I told the
driver.

My mother looked at me curiously.

"It's time for a meeting, ma."

She simply nodded her head because she knew
it was time.

I pulled out my new phone that I had just
bought and sent a text to Blaze, Young, Nina, and
the rest of our crew. It was about that time, and
pregnant or not, I was ready to finish this war.

Barbie Scott
TRAP GYRL 3

***

Sitting at the head of the table, directly across from my mother, I waited patiently for Young Larry and Capri to join us. Blaze walked in with his Bonnie (Tiny) followed by Nina and Carlos. Marcus was already in the back going in on his laptop, digging up any and everything he could find on Mario. I knew it would be hard getting to Mario but I would be sure to hit him where it hurts; his family.

"Man, did yall see that knockout punch Ms. Lopez put on Nathine's old ass," Blaze said, punching the air for demonstration. As bad as I didn't want to laugh, I couldn't help it. Blaze was a fucking fool. "Ms. Lopez, I'ma start calling you Ms. Guadalupe Ali," Blaze joked, and we all laughed.

"I hate that I had to do that but yall know I don't play over my baby," my mother said in her half-broken English. "Oh, we know," Young shot, smirking and again we all laughed.

After about fifteen minutes, the rest of the crew walked in and took their seats. Now, it was time to get down to business.

"I'm more than sure everyone knows why we're here," I spoke.

Everyone nodded.

Barbie Scott
TRAP GYRL 3

"The Carlito's have violated us in the worst way. Niya's dead, and not to mention all the other bodies that were laid out. We all know how hard it is to get to Mario. So, for now, we're gonna start with his crew. I want them all dead, one by one and, his younger son kidnapped. We won't kill him but when his crew comes to get him, we will kill them. I want his wife dead and anyone else associated to the Carlito's. No Kids! Young, do you hear me?" I looked over at Young. "No Kids!" I exclaimed.

Young was a real hot head. He was the type to shoot mother's, grannies, kids, and anyone else in his way. True, I was a real Gutta Gyrl but killing kids wasn't in me.

"Yes, Ms. Cash, I hear..."

He spoke but was cut short. He looked towards the door along with everyone else. As if on cue, we all pulled out our burners and watched the front door closely. I sighed at the sight of Que. He walked in with his arm bandaged and slightly limping. I jumped from my seat and ran over to him.

"Oh my God, Que!" I couldn't stop smiling.

He looked up at me and smiled weakly.

"Mijo!" my mother shouted, running over to us.

TRAP GYRL 3

Everyone cheered him on as he walked slowly over to the table and took his normal seat.

Right when I went to sit down, an excruciating pain ran through my stomach, causing me to bend over. I had been having pains lately but not like the one I was experiencing at this very moment. A gush of water began to run down my legs and I began to panic.

"Ms. Cash, you're peeing on yourself?" Young asked with an astonished look.

"Nigga, her water just broke," Blaze said and stood to his feet.

"Oh, my, Cash." Nina ran over to me and began rubbing my back.

"Ahhh!" I screamed out. The pain was unbearable.

"Come on, Cash we gotta get you to the hospital," my mother said.

I walked towards the door slowly. When I looked back at Tiny and Nina, they both wore a frantic look and it only made me more nervous.

Please let my baby be ok, I thought to myself walking out to the limo.

Chapter III

Que

I guess my surprise entrance made Cash go into labor. I laughed to myself once I saw that her water had broke. Blaze had told me there was a meeting going on so I left the hospital. I was tired of being in that bitch. I had shit to do and being in the hospital was blocking my flow. The nurses told me I wasn't in any condition to leave, but fuck that, I had to go. I had plenty money so I would just hire a private nurse to take care of me.

I missed my daughter like a muthafucka and I needed to find the muthafuckas that shot me and Bree. Baby girl was in there fighting for her life and that shit was killing me. I was thankful she was still alive but at any giving moment, Nino would probably want to pull the plug. I swear, on my life, if she woke up from her coma, I would stop my hoeish ways and be the man she needs me to be. I

Barbie Scott
TRAP GYRL 3

would do anything in my power to convince Nino I love her and I won't hurt her.

Driving home, I couldn't help but think of Bree, and listing to this damn song was making shit harder for me.

This what happens when I think about you
I get in my feelings, yeah
I start reminiscing, yeah
Next time around, fuck I want it to be different, yeah
Waiting on a sign, guess it's time for a different prayer
Lord, please save her for me, do this one favor for me
I had to change my player ways, got way too complicated for me
I hope she's waiting for me

A nigga wanted to break down just hearing the lyrics. I was fucked inside. Flashes of Bree's face when she got that call rained heavy on my mind. The look she wore said that something was wrong but I never got a chance to find out who was the caller. She began crying and next thing I knew, shots rang out. When I looked over at her, her dress was covered in blood. No lie, I thought I had lost her. Shit, I thought I was gone too.

Cash had told me how the wedding got shot up so I guess it wasn't meant for us to make it to the chapel. The sound of my phone ringing knocked me out my train of thoughts. Seeing that it was Esco, I quickly answered.

"Sco, what's up?"

"Que, who the hell you think you are, 2pac, my guy?" Esco laughed, referring to me checking myself out the hospital.

"Man, I had to get out that bitch."

"Where are you now? Can you come to mi casa? I really need to rap with you."

"I'm just leaving the warehouse. Everyone went to the hospital, Cash's water broke."

"Ok, so you going up there?"

"Nah, I'm tired of that place. I told Cash I'll come after the baby is born."

"Okay... well, come by."

"Aight, I'm on my way." I disconnected the line.

I jumped on the highway and headed to Esco's mansion. Whatever he wanted to talk to me about had to be serious. I kinda figured it had something to do with the Carlito's.

When I pulled up to Esco's, I was let in by his security gate. It took me every last ounce of energy to get out the car. Scrunching from the pain, I slowly walked to the front door. It took me forever in a day to climb his stairs to his office. When I finally made it, I quickly took a seat because my stomach was killing me.

"Sup, Esco?"

"Are you ok?"

"Yeah, I'm good."

"I called you here because I wanna talk to you about Mario's daughter."

"Mario's daughter?" I asked, confused.

"Yes. The young lady you were screwing is indeed his daughter."

"Wait, what lady?"

"The young lady you brought to Nina's baby shower."

"Stephanie?" I said her name, still confused.

It all started making sense. When she approached me in my cell, she already knew everything about me. The way she approached me was slick as fuck too.

"You had no idea?" Esco shook his head.

"Hell nah. I met her when I was in jail. She's a Deputy in the county."

"Yes, so she set you up, basically."

"That bitch!" I shouted, shaking my head.

That hoe straight set me up. But what's crazy is she's pregnant by me. Why the fuck would she go so far as to letting me put a baby in her? I asked myself, furious.

I got up to leave. I couldn't wait to call this bitch.

"Que, you need to find her and handle that," Esco said with a serious look. But what he didn't know was she was pregnant with my child, how the fuck was I gonna kill her while she is pregnant?

"I'ma handle it, Sco," were my last words before walking out.

Brooklyn Nino

Doing a little over 80 MPH, I furiously drove to the hospital. Cash was in labor and she didn't bother to call me. I know I fucked up, but damn, it was my baby too. Not to mention, she was only seven months so anything could happen to my son and this bitch was being stubborn. Carlos had called me and told me she went to the hospital. And, not only that but they had a meeting without me like I didn't want to put a bullet in each and every last Carlito.

When I walked into the hospital, I went to the information desk and gave them Cash's first and last name. The nurse punched in keys on her computer then looked over at me.

"May I have your name, sir?"

"Brooklyn Carter."

"I'm sorry, sir, but your name isn't on the list."

"What the fuck you mean my name is not on the list? I'm the child's father!" I shouted, causing everyone to look in our direction.

"I understand, sir, but she has a strict list of visitors and there's no Carter on the list."

I wanted to jump over the counter and ring this bitch neck but I chose to leave peacefully.

Walking out the hospital lost, it seemed as if I was in this shit alone. I wanted to go to the trap and holla at Kellz but I thought against it. I drove out to my restaurant to have myself a much-needed drink. So much had been going on I nearly forgot about my business I had running. Thanks to my nigga Kellz, he kept my shit going and making sure my deposits were on time.

Barbie Scott
TRAP GYRL 3

When I pulled up, the place was packed, like always. I went to my bar and ordered a double shot of 1738. I knocked it back in one gulp then ordered another one. I was so in my thoughts that everything around me was mute. It seemed as if I was in the restaurant alone but that was just psychological thinking because the entire place was crowded. I looked over and noticed a chick eyeing me. She was pretty as fuck or either it was the liquor talking. I quickly turned my head and focused in on the tender who I placed another drink order with.

When I looked over again, the lady was still watching me but quickly turned her head. She looked hella familiar to me but I couldn't quite put my finger on it. I waited for her to look at me again, and when she did, I motioned her to come over to me with a head nod. She stood to her feet and sashayed over to me. I patted the seat next to me for her to have a seat. She did as told and I flagged Jesse, my bartender, back over.

"Jesse, let me get another shot and give the young lady one also," I said then looked at her for any signs of objection.

"Mr. Carter, are you gonna be ok? You've had quite a few drinks," Jesse said.

TRAP GYRL 3

I shot him a look that said do as told, and without another word, he walked off.

"Excuse me, I didn't get your name?"

"I'm sorry." she extended her hand. "I'm Arcelie," she responded, batting her eyes.

"I'm Nino." I gave her a half smile.

"Nice to meet you." She smiled back.

Jesse walked over and sat the drinks in front of us.

"So, are you here alone?" I asked her.

"Um, yes. I come here to have a drink all the time."

"Oh, ok. So, where's your man?"

"I don't have one."

"You mean a pretty girl like you ain't got a nigga? That's kinda hard to believe."

"Well, believe it, because it's the truth," she said, bashfully.

Her shyness was kinda cute. I know now wasn't the time to be entertaining another woman, but shit, Cash was done with me. It's been a little over a month and I ain't had no pussy. I mean, damn, I am a man.

The liquor was taking control over me, I discreetly slid my hand up her red dress. When she didn't object, I went up further finding her panties.

Barbie Scott
TRAP GYRL 3

Oh yeah, she's a thot, I thought to myself as I used one finger to slide her panties to the side.

Here we were, in the middle of a restaurant, and this bitch was letting me play with her pussy. If that didn't scream thot then there had to be a much worst name for it.

I pulled my hand from under her dress and led her towards the back. She hesitantly walked with me as I led her into my office. Quickly, I locked the door then walked up to her, picking her up off her feet.

"Umm, Brooklyn, I don't want you to think I'm some sort of hoe."

I stopped in my tracks and looked at her with a confused look on my face.

How the fuck she know my name is Brooklyn? I asked myself then brushed it off.

"I don't think you a hoe, ma. Shit, we're grown, and if we both want this, then why would I judge you?" I lied straight through my teeth.

I slid her panties off and flung them across my office. I went into my drawer and pulled out a magnum condom. I tore the wrapper open using my teeth then slid it on. I tried to slid in her but she pushed me back.

"What's up, ma?" I asked her.

TRAP GYRL 3

She dropped to her knees and began sucking me up. I had to hold onto my desk because this bitch was sucking the life out of me.

Damn! I thought as I bit my bottom lip. She was indeed a freak.

I grabbed her head and began pumping in and out her mouth like I was in her pussy. She had a steady rhythm going and not gagging once. After sucking me up for some time, she pulled me over to my sofa and laid me down. She then climbed on top of me and eased down on my dick. She began bouncing up and down like she been missing my dick for some time. I didn't know this girl but I was sure to hit her off again; and soon.

After I busted a fat nut, I sent ol' girl on about her way. She stored her number into my phone and I promised to give her a call. I hopped in my whip then pulled out my phone and called Blaze. I needed to check on Cash and the baby.

"Yooo?" Blaze answered.

"Sup, man. How is she doing?"

"Well, you're officially a daddy, nigga. She had a boy."

"Hell yeah," I said, smiling hard as a muthafucka. "How's his condition?"

TRAP GYRL 3

"Well, he's good. He was only four pounds so they wanna keep him in for a couple weeks."

"I'm just glad he's ok," I sighed. "Man, Cash is a trip, she didn't put me on the visiting list."

"I'ma holla at her, man, don't trip."

"Good looking, Blaze."

"Fasho, Nino. I'm about to head home, now. It's work that needs to be done in the streets," Blaze said, and I already knew what he meant.

"I'm about to head to the house too. Make sure you hit me up, though, because shit gotta get handled."

"Aight, one."

"One."

We hung up.

I turned up my music and headed home. I was gonna get some rest but after tomorrow, I was going on a killing spree. I promised myself I won't rest until I get at least five bodies this week.

Chapter IV

Cash Lopez

It had been a week since I had seen Brooklyn, and every day that went by, I missed him more and more. Now, just because I missed his ass that didn't mean I wanted him back. As of right now, I didn't want shit to do with him. Everyone said I was overreacting, but no one was in my shoes to understand how I felt. Deep down inside, I knew that it was a possibility for us to get back together, but for now, it was *fuck him.*

After my healing process, I was going to work on getting my figure back, and then find me a boo to dick me down and keep it pushing. It's been one week since I had BJ, Brooklyn Jr., and I was already losing this pudge in my stomach. The way I was feeling, I was at a point of no return, so a relationship was the last thing I was worried about; I was going back to the old me.

Barbie Scott
TRAP GYRL 3

In the meantime, I was at home suiting up, I needed to pay someone a surprise visit. After I made my surprise visit, I was heading to the hospital to check on my baby boy. Slipping into my black Pro Club T-shirt, my black Jordan tights, and my all black Jordan 12's, I was ready. I went to my closet and grabbed my twin Berettas out of my safe. Of course, Dolly was strapped to my ankle. *Old faithful. She's been here longer than these niggas.*

When I reached the bottom of my steps, my mother was sitting at the table counting money on her money counter. She looked at me as if she was studying me. She eyed my attire from head to feet. The stern look she was giving me let me know that she knew I was out for vengeance. The faint pause between us was my cue to walk out. I quickly hopped into my black Spider and pulled out into the foggy night air. I had so much on my mind, I chose not to listen to any music. I needed to focus because if I slipped up, I'd be dead before I made it in.

When I pulled up to the large white gated home, I parked up the street under a huge palm tree that shaded my car from the moonlight. From where I sat, I had a perfect view of the home. It was finally time to put some of my tactics to use that Pedro had taught me in my adolescence days. I loved Pedro, dearly. He was the one that taught me how to shoot and even the Martial Art tactics I knew. Pedro was there when I caught my first body, and he never told a soul.

"Hey, Cash," Marco said, coming into my bedroom. I was only 10 years old, sitting at my vanity playing with my dolls. My mother, and whom I thought was my father, had left for a meeting so I was left alone with our homes staff.

"Hi, Marco. You wanna play with me? My Mommy bought me a new Ken doll."

"Si, mija. I'll love to play dolls with you," he responded and took a seat on the floor in front of me.

He picked up the dolls and began playing with them causing me to burst out into a laughter. After about 15 minutes of playing with the dolls, his hand began to wonder underneath my dress. I froze still in my seat, not knowing how far he would go. He used his one finger to pull my panties to the side, but using his elbows to open my legs wider. To say I was beyond scared would be an understatement. This was the man I looked up to, this was my mother's dear friend and one our top security. I was so scared, but because of what I was about to do.

Barbie Scott
TRAP GYRL 3

"I have another pretty baby doll you wanna see?"

"Yes, mija, let me see," he spoke slowly with his mouth half opened as if he was enjoying himself under my dress.

"Ok, but it's a surprise, you have to close your eyes," I giggled to hide my fear.

I made him put his hands over his eyes as I lifted from my seat. I slid my tiny hands under my mattress and retrieved the .22 automatic my mother had given me. No one knew I had it. I pointed it to the back of his head and without warning, I pulled the trigger. He slowly turned around with a frightened look. He reached out to grab me but I quickly stepped back. His body fell face forward as I watched his eyes roll to the back of his head.

"Oh my God, Cash!" Pedro shouted, running into my room. He grabbed the gun out of my hands and pulled me out into the hallway.

I looked back once more before I followed Pedro, and Marco's eyes were open. I watched as the blood poured from his head and onto my plush gray carpet. Pedro looked me in the eyes and at that very moment, he figured why I had done it.

Barbie Scott
TRAP GYRL 3

He spoke just above a whisper. "I'll handle it, mi amor. Go clean yourself up," he said, and quickly hopped on the phone.

I had caught my first body and Pedro cleaned up my mess.

From that day, he began training me on how to kill and clean up the mess. He also gave me fighting lessons and much more.

The bright headlights coming towards me knocked me out of my train of thoughts. I quickly ducked down as the car passed by me. I exit my car and quietly crept across the street to the high fenced gate. It appeared to be about 50 feet tall but that was nothing to a savage.

***

"Hello, Julio?"

"How the fuck you get in mi casa?" He jumped up from the position he was laying in. The look he wore was a scared one. He knew what I was capable of just like I knew if he could he'd kill me as well.

"It don't matter, puto! You know why I'm here."

"Cash, please, Mija, don't do this."

Barbie Scott
TRAP GYRL 3

"Oh, now you begging, Julio?" I asked with a stern look. "Just tell me where I can find Stephanie."

"I don't know. I swear, I don't! Mario cut her off the moment he found out that she was having a baby by the negro," he said, referring to Que.

"Baby?"

"Yes, Stephanie is pregnant by Que, Cash. Mario sent her to his cell in jail to seduce him. She fell in love with him and got pregnant. Now, Mario doesn't want anything to do with her," Julio spoke in his broken English.

I couldn't believe what he was saying. *Pussy is gonna be the death of that boy*, I thought to myself, thinking of Que's many flings.

"Please, don't kill me," Julio cried out, snapping me out my daze.

"Awe, poor Julio. I would have spared you, but you're a trader. And, the Lopez's don't fuck with traders," I spoke with much vengeance.

I pulled my Nesmuk Slicer from my waist and eyed him, widely.

"Ohh no, please," he cried out.

I positioned myself behind him and sliced him across the throat from ear to ear. Once I was satisfied, I pushed his body off me and retrieved his cell phone from the nightstand. I would give it to Marcus to trace all in and outgoing numbers. I walked over to the window and slipped into the darkness, as quietly as I came. My mission was complete.

Julio was one of my mother's soldiers many years ago. The only man she pretty much trusted with her life was Julio, Marco, and Pedro. Marco knew everything about our operation from the account info to the safe houses. Thanks to Esco, he alerted my mother of Julio working with Mario so my mother was able to change locations and security codes. Soon, he became alert that my mother knew of his betrayal. He fled and began working as Mario's full-time employee.

After riding around in such deep thoughts, I began missing my baby. After dealing with such a horrific memory, BJ was the only one at this point that could calm my nerves. I headed home to rid myself of my vindictive acts and making sure to scrub every part of my body good. Once I was done, scrubbing Julio's blood off me I began dressing in something comfortable then made my way to the hospital.

When I walked into the nursery, Brook was leaning over feeding BJ in his incubator.

Barbie Scott
TRAP GYRL 3

Shit! I cursed myself because this was the last person I wanted to see.

"How did you get in here?" I questioned, slipping on my cap and gloves.

"Fuck you mean? This my fucking baby too, Cash."

"I don't give a fuck. Shouldn't you be downstairs with your bitch?" I shouted.

"Man, that ain't my bitch," he spoke, sounding ashamed. "Man, look, Cash… can we go home and talk, please?"

"Talk? Nigga, ain't shit to talk about! I don't want shit to do with you. And, as for my baby, you'll see him when he's walking and talking, nigga."

The moment after I said that, he ran up into my space. His chest was heaving up and down as if he wanted to smack me.

"I swear, you play with my fucking son, you won't make it out alive to see his first birthday."

"Is that a threat or a promise, Nino," I said meeting his stare.

I stepped even closer to him to show him I wasn't scared one bit. He looked down at me and his face softened. I brushed that shit off and turned my back to him. I didn't have shit else to say. I

TRAP GYRL 3

walked over to the window and looked out into the night. Moments later, I could hear Brooklyn's footsteps walking away from where I stood and when I heard the door shut, I knew he had left. I sighed in relief because I didn't want to fall putty in his hands. I was horny, I missed him, and not to mention, he was fine as a muthafucka.

I sat down on the chair that was near BJ's incubator. I reached inside and began rubbing the top of his head but making sure to be gentle with his soft spot. I knew he was gonna be spoiled, but hey, this was my first baby, so I really didn't care. I had to admit, it felt great to be a mother. I had someone in this world that I knew would love me unconditionally and never turn his back on me. For him to have been so small, he already had Brooklyn's features. The only thing that he had of mines was my big doe shaped eyes.

His tiny finger held tightly onto my index finger for dear life. I kissed the top of his head over and over, I couldn't help but think about Brook. I hated what was going on between us and I was starting to miss him something serious. The moment I thought of him, I also thought about Tiffany being downstairs and she was also pregnant with his baby. I got pissed in an instant. I understood that Brook needed me right now because he was going through it about Bree, but I couldn't get over the fact he was sharing a child with a bitch that was a supposedly jump off.

The sound of my ringing phone caused me to look down. I quickly answered so it wouldn't awaken BJ.

"Hello?"

"Sup, Cash?"

"Carter?" I asked, puzzled. It had been over a month and this nigga was just now reaching out.

"Yeah, baby girl, it's me," he said, sounding a bit intoxicated.

"Oh my God, where have you been? So much has been going on, Crater!"

"I know, ma. I'm in Brazil right now. Some shit happened out here at one of my traps. Lydia told me what happened to Bree," he said and sighed. "How's she holding up?"

"She's in a coma but she'll pull through."

"I hope, man. But, aye, I'ma check back in with you soon, alright?"

"Yes," I spoke, on a verge of crying. "Carter?" I called out to him.

"Yeah, baby girl."

"Be safe, ok?"

TRAP GYRL 3

"Always, ma…" and with that, he hung up.

Something in his voice told me he was worried about something. When he didn't show up to the wedding, I figured he was still a little jealous because I was marrying Brooklyn. The one thing I hated the most was this whole thing started because of him, and here it was, he left us to deal with it alone.

Chapter V

Que

"**H**ello?" Stephanie answered the phone, surprisingly.

"Bitch, you know I'ma kill you, right?"

"Que, I'm so sorry." She began to cry.

"You set me up this whole time."

"I swear, I didn't, Que. I promise."

"Bitch, tell me the truth!" I demanded.

"When I first approached you in jail, I was sent by my father. He asked me to get close to you. I really didn't mean to fall in love with you, but it happened," she continued to cry. "I fell in love with you, Quintin!"

"You don't love me! You a snake, yo! My fucking girl laying up in the hospital because of your fucking father!"

TRAP GYRL 3

"My father didn't shoot you, Que. I will admit, he shot up the wedding but he didn't shoot you," she began crying harder.

I looked at the phone in disbelief. This hoe was lying.

"Que, I need you. My father cut me off after he found out I was pregnant," she pleaded.

"Nah, hoe. I ain't fucking with you. I'm through with yo' snake ass."

"What about my baby?"

"Exactly, yo' baby!" I shouted and hung up.

I was done with Stephanie's bitch ass. Fuck her and her baby. It was bad enough I was fucking with a pig, but her being Mario's daughter was icing on the cake. Her telling me the Carlito's did not shoot me and Bree reigned heavy on my mind but it didn't matter because she had admitted it was them that shot up the wedding. Stephanie was a dead bitch, pregnant or not. I couldn't wait to get a hold of her. But right now, I needed to see Bree.

***

When I pulled up to the hospital, I took the elevator up to Bree's room. I hated to see her like this and that's what kept me away. I walked into her room and took a seat beside her bed. The more I stared at her, the more I became upset. Seeing her hooked up to all these machines was killing a nigga. Though she looked peaceful, I knew she was suffering. Even with the scar across the side of her face from where the glass had shattered, she was still beautiful.

"Girl, I'm glad you got good hair cause that shit all over the place," I said, tryna make myself laugh. It was like the sound of my voice made a connection with her because her heart monitor began to speed up, so I continued to talk to her.

"Yeah, baby, it's daddy," again, I laughed. "All bullshit aside, Bree, a nigga miss the shit out of you. I can't sleep, I barely could eat, ma. And, I know I'll never be the same until you recover from this. It's crazy how yo' ass just came around and changed a nigga. I ain't gone lie, I was a player by nature," again, I laughed. "But, you changed that, baby. I swear, if you make it out of this, I'ma change my playa ways. It's gonna be me and you. I swear, if something goes wrong, I'ma kill everybody associated, hell, I might even kill myself. I can't see my life without you, baby girl."

I lifted from the chair and walked over to her bedside. I closed my eyes and wished like a

TRAP GYRL 3

muthafucka that she would open hers. Of course, that was wishful thinking. A lone tear slipped from my eye, and right then, I knew I loved this girl.

"I love you, Breelah Carter," I said before leaving the room. I walked to the door but looked back one last time before leaving. I needed my baby to wake up soon or I was going to lose it

By the time I made it home, I was in so much pain. All I wanted to do was lay down and relax, but I knew I couldn't with this bitch Keisha here. Ever since I had gotten shot, she came to stay at my house with my daughter. She thought, because she was here, we would be back together, but fuck no; wasn't shit happening. Little did she know, the moment Bree woke up from her coma, I was taking my daughter and kicking her ass out.

I was really going to make shit official with Bree. I was through with the games and tired of these hoes. I knew eventually I was gonna wife baby girl all I needed was Nino's blessings. Since all this shit had been going on, I haven't heard a peep from Carter's punk ass. I knew that nigga wasn't built for this shit, he pretty much let the Cartel run his ass out the state. Ol pussy ass nigga.

When I walked into the house, it was pitch black. I searched the entire downstairs before going upstairs to find Keisha and Qui. When I walked upstairs, Qui wasn't in her room so I went to search my room.

"What the fuck!" I shouted the minute I walked through the door.

Keisha was on the bed passed out and Qui was sitting on the floor in a diaper. When I ran over to her, I noticed white residue around her mouth and a plate sitting on the side of her. I began to panic. I whacked Keisha across her face right before I picked my daughter up.

"Ouch, nigga!" Keisha screamed, holding her jaw.

"Bitch, your dope head ass in my house snorting and shit. My fucking daughter got this shit all around her mouth!" The moment I said it, Qui began choking. Her eyes were bloodshot red and she didn't look good. I laid my baby down and began to punch Keisha, repeatedly. My daughter was crying hysterically and I knew it was from the dope.

"I'm sorry, Que. I'm sorry," this bitch was screaming.

"Nah, hoe, you gone really be sorry if something happens to my baby."

I scooped up Qui and rushed outside to the car.

Barbie Scott
TRAP GYRL 3

Man, what the fuck I'ma tell these people? I thought about what the fuck was I about to tell the hospital.

I strapped Qui in her car seat and then hopped in. For the second time today, I cried. It seemed like my life was getting worse by the day.

When I made it to the hospital, I rushed the nurses counter. Qui was still crying, non-stop, but I figured I'd tell them she swallowed something.

"I need to see a doctor Patrice!" I shouted to the front desk nurse. Patrice was one of my old jump off's I had to cut loose because she was getting too clingy. She always had Cash's name in her mouth, that was another thing, and anybody that knew me knew I don't play when it came to Cash Lopez.

"Hey, Que," she said, flirtatiously, which was about to annoy my fucking soul.

"Pee, my baby swallowed some… some, Ajax, please get her to a doctor!"

"Oh my God!" She jumped from her seat.

She quickly grabbed Qui and began taking her vital signs. Once she was done, she began paging the doctors. After about ten minutes, three doctors had come and rushed Qui upstairs.

TRAP GYRL 3

After a few hours of waiting, I sent Cash a text because I knew she was more than likely upstairs.

Me: Man, you ain't gonna believe this shit, Wifee.
Wifee: What's wrong, Que?
Me: You at the hospital?
Wifee: Yeah, I'm here with BJ.
Me: Come downstairs. I'm on the 3rd floor in the hallway soon as you get off the elevator
Wifee: ok I'm on my way down now

When Cash finally made it down, she had a frightened look on her face. So much had been going on in our lives, it was like a family curse. When she made it to me, her eyes looked distraught like she was ready to cry. All I could do was shake my head and put it down.

"What happened?" she asked with pleading eyes.

"Man, I got home and this bitch, Keisha, was passed out in my room. Qui was on the floor next to the plate, Cash," I said, shaking my head. "She had dope residue all over her mouth," I spoke, sounding ashamed.

"Oh, my... so, what did you tell the hospital?"

TRAP GYRL 3

"I told them she swallowed Ajax…"

Right then, a doctor walked up to us.

"Mr. Johnson, I'm Dr. Pollard, and this is Ms. Garcia, she's with DCFS."

The moment the doctor said that the lady with him was a social worker, I knew what that meant. My eyes instantly got watery and I was ready to break down.

"Mr. Johnson, we found narcotics in your daughter's system. It has increased her sense of alertness, reduced her appetite, and she has a rapid heartbeat. Other than that, she's is going to live. However, she'll be placed in foster care until you complete the necessary steps to get her back."

It seemed like everything he said after foster care was a blur. Right then, three officers headed towards Qui's room, followed by the social worker from DCFS. I reached for my gun, and Cash quickly grabbed me.

"What the fuck you doin', nigga? Your bout to get us all killed!" Cash was in my face shouting. A nigga straight started crying like a bitch.

"Mr. Johnson, I know you're upset, but please, relax. Right now, you're really lucky they're not arresting you for child endangerment," the doctor said just above a whisper. He turned to walk away

TRAP GYRL 3

and I was left stuck with so much hatred towards everybody in the hospital.

"I'm about to kill this bitch!"

I stormed out the hospital to my car. I sped home doing 100. I prayed Keisha was there because right now that bitch was dead.

When I made it home, I stormed into the house, trying to find this hoe. I searched high and low but the bitch was nowhere to be found. I began calling her phone and not once did she answer. I jumped back in my whip and headed to her mother's house because that's the only place she could have went.

When I made it there, I jogged to the door, and Ms. Sanders answered. I pushed past her and started searching the house. I looked in closets, under beds, and every bathroom in the house. Again, that bitch wasn't there.

"Que, what's going on?" Ms. Sanders asked, walking into the bathroom.

I looked at her and shook my head.

"They took Qui, Ms. Sanders," I began to cry again.

"Who took her, baby? Talk to me."

"DCFS. She swallowed some dope, ma."

After I said that, her eyes bulged like she seen a ghost.

Barbie Scott
TRAP GYRL 3

"Your dope head ass daughter was getting high while my daughter was right there."

Ms. Sanders just looked at me and within seconds, her face was buried in tears.

I sat down on the bathtub and Ms. Sanders began to rub my back. I ran my hands down my face and like a baby, I buried my head into Ms. Sanders chest and we cried together.

Chapter VI

Brooklyn Nino

The other day, I stood by the door to my sister's room and heard Que pouring his heart out to her next to her hospital bed. That shit stressed me out more. I knew what kind of nigga he was, but in my time of knowing Que, I never heard or seen him cry. Everything he said sounded so sincere. I didn't know if I was just tripping, but right now, I needed Bree to wake up because that nigga seemed like he was losing himself over her. I hated my sister and Que were dating but maybe the nigga did change his hoe ways. Maybe he really does love my sister. Just like Cash and I. Cash was a bonafide player and swore she wouldn't ever be with one nigga. she was fucking Me, Que and even Ricky bitch ass. I didn't hold it against her, I just prayed I could change her little hoeish ass ways, and it worked. I understood that change was possible. Maybe Bree was changing Que and maybe he would be a good nigga to her. So, for now, I was going to back up and let him love her. But the minute he fucks over her, he's dead.

You need some loving, Big Daddy?" My lady friend walked up and straddled my lap. She began kissing my ears and then worked her way down my chest. Ever since the night at my restaurant, we had been texting each other. Cash wasn't giving a nigga any play so I had to hit this bitch off until my wife lets me come back home.

She thought that I didn't know she was home with my son, but soon as the hospital released them, Blaze had reached out to me. The day I had walked out the hospital, I didn't go back. I had paid one of the nurses two g's to keep me updated on BJ's condition and when she informed me he had gained four pounds, I knew he would be free to go home. I was going to make a surprise visit to Cash's house but I didn't want to be rejected. Even if we never got back together, she wasn't going to keep my little nigga away from me. This was my first child, not to mention, he's a Junior. He was still tiny as fuck so I was going to give him time to grow. The minute he could hold his head up on his own, I was going to kick the door down, strong arm Cash, and take my little nigga with me.

Barbie Scott
TRAP GYRL 3

"Damn!" I yelled out like a straight hoe.

This bitch knocked me out my whole train of thought the way she was sucking on my dick. She was rough with it but in a seductive kind of way. I looked down and her head was bobbing up and down with a steady rhythm. I grabbed her head and guided it because I was on a verge of nutting already.

"Damn, Cash! Right there, bae."

Did I just call the bitch... yes, I did, I thought to myself?

She stopped and looked up at me. I pushed her head down because I didn't give two fucks. I exploded right in her mouth. She swallowed every last drop and lifted up. The look she wore, told me she was mad but I didn't give a fuck. I got up and went to the shower.

Right when I hopped in, she barged through the door. "So, you calling me yo wife name?" she asked, walking over to the sink.

How does this bitch know that's my wife? I thought to myself.

I ignored her and grabbed the bar of Irish Spring soap and began soaping my washcloth.

Barbie Scott
TRAP GYRL 3

"You could let yourself out, ma," I said, and turned back around to and started washing my body.

She stormed out, so I figured she was leaving.

I didn't give a fuck, I needed to do a pop up on Cash and BJ.

I jumped out the shower and went to my closet. I pulled out some Saint Laurent Jeans and a white V-Neck Tee. I threw on my red and white Jordan 4s, and I was ready. My hair needed to be re-dreaded but I was still a fly nigga so my swag made up for it.

First, I went to the mall. I bought BJ six pairs of Jordan's, size one, and ten boxes of Jordan outfits. I then went to Zale's and copped him some 5 karat diamond earrings. After that, I went into Nordstrom's and got him some True Religion jeans. My little man was about to be on. I had a custom necklace made for Cash with his hospital pictures in it, I just prayed she would accept it.

After I was done in the mall, I went to my trap house to holla at Kellz. I needed to get my dough and make my deposits. I knew after I was done with my day, I'd be tired. I just hoped when I got to Cash's house, I could relax. Knowing her, she would trip, but I didn't care because I'd simply go into Ms. Lopez's room and max out. Ms. Lopez loved a nigga so she wouldn't trip.

***

I stepped out my car and opened my trunk to retrieve the items for BJ. I prepared myself for Cash and her bullshit. The last time I saw her was at the hospital. She wigged out on me but her eyes told me a different story. She wanted a nigga in the worst way. That's exactly why I was showing up and looking good. Hopefully, she'd stop tripping and bust that pussy open for a real nigga.

"Hahaha," I laughed to myself as I walked up to the door.

I looked through the tiny glass windows and didn't see a soul so I walked through the side gate that led to the patio and backyard. When I got to the patio, Ms. Lopez and Pedro was sitting on their usual bench, right in front of the water fountain.

These two are always plotting.

I laughed to myself because I was around long enough to know that this was their spot whenever they were plotting.

"Nino, como estas?" Pedro said, in his language.

TRAP GYRL 3

"Soy buen, Pedro," I replied, with my broken Spanish. Being around them, I had picked up on a lot of Spanish.

"Hey Nino" Ms. Lopez cooed smiling wide. I could tell she was happy to see a nigga and that shit made me feel good inside.

"Sup, ma? What you and Pedro out here plotting on?" I laughed, causing them to laugh also.

"Oh, you know us. Bodies, Mijo," Ms. Lopez said with a smirk. But I knew she was dead serious.

Bodies. I laughed to myself, again. Little did she know, I had a few missions of my own.

After the wedding, I had sent Kellz and my crew to holla at the Cartel. I was so busy, back and forth to the hospital, dealing with BJ and Bree, I was lost. Fuck them small time niggas, I wanted Mario; straight up.

"Ms. Lopez, is Cash here?"

"Yes, Mijo you know where to find her," she laughed.

I walked through the second gate and just like Ms. Lopez said, her ass was right where I could find her.

When I made it to the back yard, I stood back and watched as Cash was swimming, what would be her last lap. The minute she looked up, I knew she would stop dead in her tracks.

Damn, her ass looking good, I thought as I watched her ass flopped in and out the water.

She was wearing a Dashiki two piece that exhilarated her skin tone.

"Fuckkk, my baby momma is bad," I mumbled. She had her little music playing and I noticed a glass on the concrete above.

I could tell you was analyzing me, I could tell you was criticizing me.

I could tell you was fantasizing that you would come slide in me and confide in me...

He could tell that I was wifey material.

He was liking my style in my videos.

I wasn't looking for love I was looking for a buzz.

So, at times I would lie and say I'm busy, yo...

Cause it's too much, and it's too clutch.

Who wants rumors of the two of us.

But when you're away, I can't get you out of my mind.

But what if I'm not the one and you're wasting your time?

But, you waited!

Barbie Scott
TRAP GYRL 3

Anybody, anybody want to buy a heart?
Anybody, anybody wanna buy love?

I listened to the lyrics and I couldn't lie, I was lost in the sauce. In a sense, it made me smile but I felt like shit. She finally looked up and our eyes met. She grabbed her towel and began drying her face and hair. She then swam to the stairs and climbed out the pool. She dried herself off but looked at me with so much hatred.

Damn! I thought to myself as I walked closer towards her. As bad as I wanted to grab her and pull her into my arms, I kept it gangsta.

"Where's my son?" I asked, in my deepest tone.

"He's in the house," she challenged, walking up with her face frowned. I just looked at her and walked into the house.

I sat the items down on the kitchen counter and browsed the house for my baby. When I found him, he was being held by an older Hispanic lady that Pedro was smashing. I quickly took him from her arms then grabbed his birth cloth and through it over my shoulder. I put his pacifier in my mouth and rocked him all the way up the stairs.

When we got into BJ's room, I laid back on his bed with him, in my arms. Damn, he looked just

TRAP GYRL 3

like me already. His eyes were wide opened so I wondered if he recognized me as his father yet. I started rubbing my hands through his hair, I couldn't wait to dread his hair up.

His little ass had gotten chunky fast.

Just looking at him made me realize I missed his mother much more. I hated that I couldn't be here to help change his diapers, wake up in the middle of the night to feed him, and even watch him grow. For him to have been prematurely born, he looked normal and had grown a lot.

"Boy, what yo mama been feeding you?"

I played with my son. I kicked my shoes off and got comfortable. Next thing I knew, I had dozed off with BJ on my chest.

Chapter VII

Cash Lopez

I quickly went to my room to started getting dressed. I did exactly what Brooklyn did, which was got extra cute. I went into BJ's room and they were sound asleep. I watched them closely and they looked so peaceful. I leaned on the doorway and admired my husband. Even with his dreads all over the place and him needing a shave, he was still sexy as ever. I wanted so bad to just kiss him but when I zoomed in on his cell phone that laid beside them, I was sidetracked. I tiptoed over to the bed. I reached over them, trying not to wake them, and grabbed his phone. I went straight to his text and began to read all his messages.

A: I'm outside

Brooklyn: *aight, here I come. A?*

Who the fuck is A? I thought to myself.

I quickly entered the number into my cell.

T: can you bring me something to eat, baby daddy?

Brooklyn: *I'm busy, ma.*

TRAP GYRL 3

T: Well, I can't go grocery shopping right now so I need food.

~~Oh, so the bitch out the hospital.~~ I thought, knowing it was Tiffany. Yeah, her little baby daddy shit irked my nerves, already.

Brooklyn: I need you to help me get my wife back.

Blaze: Lil nigga, you know I got you. It's gonna be hard but I'll try, Nino.

Brooklyn: Yeah, her stubborn ass. Man, I'm ready to just tie her ass up and store her ass in my basement.

Blaze: Nigga, and have Ms. Lopez kick your door in? Ok...

Brooklyn: lol...

I couldn't help but smile at Brook and Blaze's messages. But as soon as I thought back on Tiffany's text and this mysterious *A* person, I was mad all over again. I dropped his phone right on the floor and walked out, leaving them asleep. I went downstairs and hopped in my Bent and headed to my shop.

When I walked in, business was going, as usual. There was a guy in each barber's chair and I could see Nikki over by the shampoo bowl washing a customer's hair.

TRAP GYRL 3

"Cash!" Monique shouted like she was excited to see me.

"Hey, Mo!" I half smiled, pretending right along with her.

We hugged and I quickly walked off toward Nikki. She had her back to me so I wrapped my hands around her eyes to surprise her.

"Guess who, bitch?" I smirked.

"Cash!" she shouted, turning around.

We hugged like we hadn't seen each other when in fact we had just seen each other four days ago.

"Bitch, where you going looking all cute?"

"Nowhere. I just came to pick up the deposits and then head up to Juice."

"Awe, shit. So, you turning up without me?"

"Oh my God, Nikkiii" I laughed because she knew damn well her honey ass don't turn up. "Nah, baby, just business."

"Look who just walked in," Nikki said, looking towards the door.

As I looked on, Arcelie took a seat in Monique's chair. It appeared that she was getting the side of her hair shaved off. Her and Monique appeared to be gossiping about something that I couldn't hear. The way the two were laughing, I knew it something interesting. As bad as I wanted to trip on the bitch, I left it alone because I didn't want to seem like I was still caught up in my feelings over Que.

"How are you and Brook doing, ma?" Nikki asked.

I turned from them bitches and focused my attention on her.

"Girl, I'm still not fucking with him. I just went through his phone and saw a few texts. Speaking of..." I said and pulled out my phone.

I dialed the number that was stored in Brook's phone under *A*. Of course, after two rings, a woman answered, just like I figured. But, what got me was the hello with the loud background. I looked at Arcelie, and it was evident that it was her. I rushed over to her and punched the bitch dead in her nose. She jumped from the chair and tried to rush me.

Oh, this bitch wanna fight back, I thought right before I went into a rage.

She was swinging like a fucking windmill and I tried dodging each shot. I was caught with two, and that made me really turn up. I four pieced her then karate kicked the bitch in her ribs, causing her to fall, instantly. Once I was satisfied with her, I walked up on Monique and two pieced her,

TRAP GYRL 3

knocking her into her station. She didn't even bother to fight back. She was on the floor, clutching her jaw.

I stormed off to my office to get my gun and permanent marker. When I walked back out, I held Dolly in one hand and my black permanent marker in the other. I kneeled down to the big Trap Gyrl sign that was painted into my floor. I wacked Monique's name out just like I had done all the other bitches that worked in my shop and crossed me.

I stood up and walked over to where Monique stood, with my gun. With my free hand, I wiped everything off her station down to the floor. I was done with this hoe. Arcelie had left because she knew what was best for her. I took a seat in Monique's barber chair and sat my strap on my lap. This hoe had approximately three minutes to get her shit and go.

Everybody in the shop watched on but no one dared to touch me or say anything to me. Nikki stood off to the side, daring anyone to jump bad, while she watched Monique gather her belongings. So many years, this bitch had been testing me like I wasn't the one feeding her. From fucking many of my skeezas, to Que, and now sitting with a bitch

TRAP GYRL 3

that was fucking my husband. Not to mention, these bitches was in my face laughing at me like I was some sort of a joke. With all the things going on in my life, I had no room for fuck bitches.

I knew I wasn't jumping off the handle because Brooklyn wouldn't have any bitch in his phone if he wasn't smashing. That bitch worked for me and my mother, so what business did she have with him, other than blowing his socks off? I couldn't wait to get back at his ass. I was gonna hit him where it hurts. I knew that two wrongs don't make a right, but it did make a muthafucking difference. He'd feel my pain one way or another.

"Cash, you straight?" Nikki walked up and stood in front of me.

Monique also walked up with tears in her eyes but that shit didn't faze me. The look on my face must have told it all because she quickly walked off out the door.

"I'm good, Nikki. Sometimes, you gotta cut the grass," I said, referring to the snakes that slithered in my lawn. I didn't have room for snakes so over the next few months, I'd be getting rid of them. Tiffany and Stephanie was next on my list.

Barbie Scott
TRAP GYRL 3

"Come here so I could do your hair, child. It's all over the place," Nikki said, and grabbed my hand, leading me to her chair.

***

Walking into Juice eased my mind, a little. I needed a drink and to relax after the episode at Trap Gyrl. I couldn't believe Brooklyn's punk ass crossed me. I was madder than hurt. I didn't have room for anymore hurt with him. Tiffany having a baby had already hurt me to the core. The only thing that hurt was how could something so perfect go so wrong? Me and Brook were fit for each other. It was like God had placed him on earth for me. Well, at least that's what I thought.

"Ring... Ring... Ring…" My phone was ringing, and honestly, I didn't want to even answer it. When I retrieved it from my bag, I was puzzled to whom it was because the number wasn't stored.

"Hello?" I had finally answered.

"Cash. Hi, its Lydia."

"Hey, Lydia." I was really puzzled as to why she was calling me. Last I knew, she was upset because of the video Carter's bitch sent her of Carter and I kissing.

TRAP GYRL 3

"Oh my god, Cash, I'm so worried about him. He hasn't called or anything." She began to cry.

"When was the last time you talked to him?"

"I haven't seen or talked to him since the day of the wedding." She cried harder.

I found that very strange because he had told me on the phone that Lydia was the one that told him about Bree getting shot. Now, here she was, telling me she hadn't even spoken with Carter. Something was weird about this and I was sure to find out.

"Don't cry, Lydia. I'll try and find him, ok? I'll also make sure he calls you."

"Ok. Thank you, Cash," she said, just above a whisper. I could hear the sincerity in her voice and it made me smile.

"You're welcome, hun. Talk to you later."

"Ok, bye."

I dropped my phone into my purse and headed upstairs to my normal VIP section. I had one of my waitresses go get me a bottle of Ace and a double shot of Hennessy. I took a seat on my white leather couch and propped my feet up on my coffee table that was made into a fish tank. It was something about the lights and the exotic fish swimming throughout the tank that eased my mind. I was so

TRAP GYRL 3

relaxed, I just prayed that the club would go smoothly and I didn't have to body anyone.

The waitress had come with my drinks. I sat back on the couch and began pouring my glass. The feeling of being watched came over me. I don't know from where but I could feel eyes on me. There was nobody in my section but me and two guards that stood at the entrance. I looked around to the other sections and my eyes fell onto a sexy nigga rocking all white. He watched me through a pair of the Versace frames but he was looking in my direction. He had a nice mocha complexion with waves that made him look mixed. He was tall and muscular as if he was some sort of NFL player. Just by the sparkle from his watch, I could tell he was getting it.

I never seen this nigga before. I wonder who's his supplier, I laughed to myself.

He was holding a bottle of Ace as well. There were women throughout his section but he wasn't paying them any attention because his ass was too busy eye fucking me behind them shades.

The effects of the liquor made me grow balls because I motioned him over. He didn't get up right away but I could see the smile on his face. I walked over and whispered to my security to let him in, if

TRAP GYRL 3

he came. Right when I turned to walk away, my DJ switched to Wale's *Bag of Money*, and this was one of my jams.

I slowly started dancing to myself. I pulled out my phone and began making me a Snapchat video. Out of nowhere, ol boy walked up behind me and wrapped his arms around my waist. I was taken by surprise that he jumped all in my video. I took it upon myself to make another one and he stayed positioned behind me and then dug his head into the crook of my neck. I added it to my story then saved it and added it on my Instagram too. He grabbed my hand and lead me to the couch. We sat down, but we didn't say one word to each other. He stared at me with a huge grin, which caused me to smile and blush like a schoolgirl.

"How you doing, future?" he addressed me.

"Future?" I asked, puzzled.

"Yeah, my future wife, ma," he spoke with so much confidence.

"Well, ok, future, but can I have a name before we start planning a wedding and shit?"

We both laughed.

"My bad, ma. My name Jahmiere, but everyone calls me Jah."

Barbie Scott
TRAP GYRL 3

"Ok, Jah… Well, I'm Cash, and it's nice to meet you."

Damn, this nigga is fine, I thought as he took off his shades. He reminded me of the rapper Nelly and his gold grill added to his sexiness.

The ringing of my phone snapped me out my lustful thoughts. I looked at it, and it was Brook. I pressed ignore and then focused my attention back on Jah.

BJ's Dad: *Who the fuck is this nigga you flexing with on social media?* Brooklyn text me, but I ignored him. Right when another text came through.

BJ's Dad: *Yeah, aight. I'm on my way up there. I swear, I'ma body you and that nigga!*

I threw my phone in my purse and looked back to the sexy ass nigga before me. I knew Brooklyn to well. He was indeed on his way so I got Jah's number and excused him from my section. I quickly went to my office and began gathering my deposits. After I was done, two of my guards walked me to my car and I headed home. I couldn't help but think of Jah's sexy ass. It was time for me to play in these streets since Brook was apparently doing him. I hate

73

TRAP GYRL 3

I had to cut it short with Jah but I knew not to test Brook's ass.

Chapter VIII

Breelah Carter

"How long have I been here?" I asked the doctor that was standing over me with his flashlight, examining my eyes.

Every day I laid in this hospital bed, I could hear voices. One minute I heard Brook's voice, then Cash. Then, one day, I would hear Que's voice. I also heard him crying but I couldn't wake up. I tried so hard to follow the bright light but every direction I walked into it seemed as I was getting further and further away from it. I needed to talk to Que and I needed to see Brook. I couldn't wait to be released. It was so much going on and I needed to be with my family.

"You've been here over two months. Do you remember what happened?"

"No." I lied as my eyes began to water. I knew exactly why I was here and exactly who had shot me.

TRAP GYRL 3

Oh my God, Que, I thought, wondering was he ok.

"Doc, is my boyfriend ok? His name is Quintin…"

He cut me off.

"Yes, Mr. Johnson is doing great. He actually checked himself out."

"Oh, ok."

"You've had quite a few visitors, my dear. You are very loved." He smiled, looking around my room. There were balloons, flowers, and teddy bears everywhere. "Your wounds have healed just fine. How are you feeling?"

"Well, my mouth is dry," I laughed. But, I feel ok, I guess."

"Great. You'll be released soon. We do wanna hold you for a few more days for observation then you're free to go."

"Ok, thanks."

"You're welcome. And, I'll be sure to send the nurse in with some water for you." He walked out.

I laid back in my hospital bed and began to wreck my brain on everything that happened when I got shot.

I remembered receiving the phone call from a woman telling me Que was the one that tried to kill

Barbie Scott
TRAP GYRL 3

*Bronx, which was the cause of him hiding out. I
began to cry as the caller spoke. Right when I
looked over at the car that had pulled up on side of
us.*

"Oh my God." I began to cry, hysterically. I
saw exactly who it was that shot me and I couldn't
believe it.

"Are you ok, Ms. Carter?" the nurse asked,
walking into my room.

"Yes, I'm fine." I smiled weakly.

She began rubbing my head and it only made
me break down. The Lord had been with us because
we were indeed supposed to be dead.

Several days had gone by since I had woken
up. The nurses were now making me walk on my
own. I was, to have been shot and in very bad
condition, I was doing pretty good for myself. I had
slight pain in my chest and shoulder arca but
nothing a few pills would help with. My doctor had
informed me if I made a bowel movement, I could
go home tomorrow. I asked my nurse to keep the
apple juice coming because I needed to leave this
place ASAP. It was too damn quiet and I already
had enough things on my mind. For the past few

days, I hadn't had any visits so I was sure that everyone would be ecstatic to see me.

***

Que...

I grabbed my ringing phone off the dresser. I figured it was Cash. She was probably telling me she was outside to pick up the money for the work. To my surprise, it was Keisha's bitch ass texting me.

Bitch: *I'm sorry, Que. please forgive me. I'm going to rehab, I'ma get clean.*

Que: *Bitch, you might as well say fuck that rehab because you're a dead bitch.*

Bitch: *Please, just give me another chance. I'ma get clean then we can start over and raise our daughter as a family.*

Que: *bitch, is you serious? You just keep hiding out 'cause you dead, Keisha. And, don't nobody want yo raggedy smoker pussy, bitch. You a dead hoe.*

Barbie Scott
TRAP GYRL 3

Bitch: *oh, so my pussy ragedy? Yeah, well, Nino thinks my head game is awesome. Lol.*

I know this bitch didn't say what the fuck I think she did? I thought, dropping my phone back down.

I couldn't believe what she had said. But, at the same time, Nino was probably salty over Cash so I wouldn't put shit past him.

So, every time he took Keisha money for me when I was in jail, he was fucking my BM?

Yeah, I had something for that nigga.

"Hey, Que," Cash said, walking into my room.

I was so deep in my thoughts, I didn't even hear her ass come in. I always forget that she has a key. Her and Breelah were the only two women that had a key. Before I got shot, I had given Bree a key just to show her I was real with this shit.

"Sup, Wifee?" I smiled at her sexy ass. I wanted so bad to tell her what Keisha had told me but I thought against it.

She plopped down on my bed with her sexy ass. She was wearing a sundress and her hair was laid. I could tell she had to be relaxing around the house because that was the only time she dressed down. Even dressed down, she was looking good.

I laid on the bed beside her and we both looked up at the ceiling. I had so much on my mind and I could tell she did too. Finally, I rolled over and faced her. Her beautiful face looked like she had been stressing and I understood because shit in our lives was hectic right now. I couldn't wait till all this shit was over with, then I could see Cash happy again.

I don't know what took over me, but I rubbed my hand up her dress. When she didn't stop me, I kept going. I pulled her thong down and looked her in her eyes.

"I miss this," I said, a little above a whisper and she sighed.

It was like her eyes were speaking to me. I kneeled down on the floor and pulled her to the edge of the bed.

"Que?" she called out, but I ignored her and dove into her pretty pussy, head first.

Damn, I missed this pussy, I thought as I began to feast.

When she grabbed my head, I knew I had her.

I worked my tongue in and out of her opening, making sure to catch all her juices. She began to wind her hips and that shit only made me lick harder. Her pussy tasted so good, I never wanted to stop. At first, she was tense but she had finally relaxed. Since all the shit with Tiffany and Nino, I

TRAP GYRL 3

know she hadn't been touched. She had called me and told me about the shit with Arcelie, then there was the shit with Keisha, so I was more than sure there would be no regrets by the time we were done.

"Oh my, God, Que! Ohhh, shit! I'm bout to...I'm about to… Oh my god."

"Yeah, baby, let that shit out. Let it out m…" I was cut off by a voice behind me.

"What the fuck!" I heard the voice and my heart fell into the pit of my stomach.

"Fuck!" I jumped up and ran behind her.

"Get the fuck off me, nigga!"

"Come on, Bree. It wasn't even like…"

"Nigga, how the fuck it wasn't like that? It looked like to me you had your fucking face buried in my brother wife's pussy. Get the fuck off me and don't ever speak to me again," she said and stormed off towards the door.

"Fuck!" I shouted, kicking the vase over that stood in the corner of my hallway.

"I'm sorry, Que." Cash appeared from the room. She had tears in her eyes and I hated that she was blaming herself.

"You good, Wifee," I ensured her.

Here we were, trying to get back at Nino, but nobody thought about Breelah.

TRAP GYRL 3

Damn.

I hadn't been to the hospital in a few days. Now, I wish I had because none of this shit would have ever happened.

"I think I'ma leave," Cash said with an ashamed look.

I walked into the bathroom to wash my face and brush my teeth, and a nigga was stressing harder than before. After that, I jumped in the shower and slipped into my all black. I had a mission to go on because I needed to relieve some stress. I was gonna go kill a couple of the Cartel's then head over to Breelah's house.

I had to get my baby girl back, by any means. I would plead my case, then give her some of this dope dick, and hopefully, she'd put it all behind us. I hated that she had to see that, and especially because I didn't want her hating Cash. I didn't give a fuck about her telling Nino because right now, it was fuck that nigga.

Chapter IX

Nina

Nina Cash Boutique...

So much has been going in my life that I was ready to lose my sanity. My best friend was dead and that shit was taking a toll on me. The only thing I had to smile about was my baby girl, Cashmere. Lately, me and Carlos had been doing pretty good but he had been in the streets more. I hated it because only three things came with the street life and that was death, jail, and bitches.

Speaking of, I had been getting anonymous calls lately and I knew that it could only be a bitch Carlos was fucking on. After the time I caught his ass on the stoop with that one chick, we had been doing great, up until about a month ago. I had received a picture text with some random hoe of Carlos and the girl in VIP at club Sonic, looking mighty cozy. I asked him about it and of course, he

TRAP GYRL 3

denied everything, but there was no denying when the proof was in the picture.

I was so over his games that I was actually getting ready for a blind date. Yes, I let Cash talk me into double dating with her and this new boo she had by the name of Jah. I mean, I had gotten my body back right, my nigga was cheating, so why the fuck not? What I couldn't believe was that Cash was the one who found us some new boos. I never thought in a million years Cash and Nino would go this far in a separation. As bad as I wanted them together, I hated seeing my bitch go through heartache so if this would make her happy then fuck it, I was all in.

"Damn, bitch, you gon' buy the whole store," I laughed as Cash dumped what appeared to be about thirty fucking outfits on the counter of my boutique.

"I couldn't help it, Best, you have some bomb ass shit. Now, the hard part is tryna figure out what I'ma wear for my date tonight," she smiled and began browsing through the clothes.

"Who you telling. Shit, I've worn everything in here and the next shipment doesn't come until next week," I said, and Cash burst out laughing.

"Oh my God, that don't make no damn sense, Nina."

TRAP GYRL 3

We laughed together.

I began ringing up Cash's items and she watched me closely. She knew what I was tryna do and her ass wasn't having it. Every time she bought things from my boutique, I would try and discount her but she would die every time. The last time she went crazy so I just didn't ring up a few items and when she got home, she called me. This girl was a mess.

"Cash, for real, $4,662?"

"I can't help it, ma," she giggled.

I just shook my head and began bagging her items.

"I know this boy bet not be ugly, Cash."

"Shit, who you telling. I hope my date don't turn me off. You know all it takes is one

thing to turn me off and I be done."

"I really can't believe you got a new boo."

"Well, he's not my boo yet. We'll see after this date. But who you tellin, shit, yo ass half married too."

"Was half married. I'm so over Carlos and his bullshit games."

"These niggas are just awful. I really hate that it had to come to this," Cash said and looked off into space. "Bitch, I got something to tell you,"

TRAP GYRL 3

Cash said and looked at me with a disapproving grin.

"Spill it, bitch!"

"Oh my god, I feel so bad," she said and sighed again before speaking. "Girl I went to collect from Que. You know a bitch ain't had none in months so I let him eat the poone-poone."

"You did what?" I shouted with my hand over my mouth.

"Girl, that ain't the bad part. While he eating it, guess who walked in on us?"

"Oh my," again, I held my hand over my mouth.

"Breelah."

She shook her head.

"Woaaah!"

"Girl, she looked so hurt. I feel so bad."

"Well, have you talked to her?"

"Nope. It's like, I don't know what to say. Shit, I'm surprised she hasn't told Brook yet."

"Nino gonna kill that nigga Que."

"I know, man." Cash shook her head.

For the remainder of the day, we chilled in my boutique talked about everything. Afterward, we were going to Trap Gyrl to get our hair touched up then head to my house to shower. Carlos mother

TRAP GYRL 3

had Cashmere and Cash's nanny had BJ so Cash
was just gonna shower at my house and we would
leave from there.

***

When we pulled up to the restaurant that Jah
told us to meet them at, I was more nervous than a
hooker sitting front row of a church house. So far,
all I knew was that his name was Dez, he was 28
years old, he had no kids, and he owned a studio.
When we got out of the car, the valet driver went
and parked, so we made our way in. We walked to
the hostess desk and she led us to our party.

When we made it near the table, I stopped and
grabbed Cash's hand to stop her from walking.

"Bitch, he is fine!" I laughed in Cash's ear,
causing her to giggle.

From the description she had given me, I knew
that the Nelly look alike was her boo. My new boo
looked a little like The Game. He was about the
same height, same body structure, and even his hair
cut. We walked over to the table and both men
stood to their feet's.

"Okay, I see we got some gentlemen on our
team, Nina," Cash said, smiling.

Both men started laughing as Jah pulled Cash in for a hug.

"How you doin, ma. I'm Dez," he spoke with that sexy ass voice.

"I'm Nina, it's nice to meet you."

"Aye, Jah, good looking. She sexy as a muthafucka" Dez looked over at Jah.

We all took our seat and the conversation began.

Every now and then, I would sneak a peek over at Cash. Whatever Jah was saying, it had her cheesing. She looked so happy but I knew it was all an act. She loved Nino, and no man could make her as happy as he did. I loved them together. Just because I ended up with a hoe ass nigga and my home wasn't happy, didn't mean I wanted Cash to give up on her and Nino's love. In my eyes, they were perfect. True, Jah seemed cool and I knew she was hurt behind Nino's and Tiffany's baby, but I still had faith that they would work past this.

Blaze & Tiny...

"Bae, is that her?" I woke Tiny up and gave her a head nod towards our prey. We had been scoping the scenery for about three hours and she had finally pulled up.

"Yeah, that's her," Tiny said and reached for her strap.

"Wait, ma. We gonna give her time to go into the house."

We watched her closely as she went to her trunk, grabbed a few bags, and then closed it. She then went to the back door and opened it. She pulled out a pink car seat and secured it around the cuff of her arm. She walked up to the front porch and sat everything down so she could open the door.

Once she was inside, Tiny and I got out the car and slowly crept towards the house. Through the tiny window, I could see her in the kitchen. She was putting up a few groceries and the car seat was on the table.

1, 2, 3...

We kicked the door in and ran in with our burners out. She didn't even get a chance to run. I snatched her ass up and walked towards the door.

"Please, can you just get my baby?" she cried out.

I looked at Tiny, and of course, her emotional ass eyes pleaded for us to get the baby. Tiny walked over and grabbed the car seat off the table. We headed out the house to the car. We put the baby in the front seat and I jumped in the back with the woman.

"Go to the hospital so we could drop the kid off," I told Tiny as she drove.

"Please, don't kill me," the lady said with tears in her eyes. It was like she knew she was about to die. If it was up to me, I'd be killing her and her baby so they could be together, but Cash strictly said, *No Kids*.

About fifteen minutes of driving, we had reached the hospital. I looked over at the lady who looked scared as fuck.

"Get out and sit the car seat on the ground. If you do any funny shit, your baby is dead."

She nodded her head, letting me know that she understood, then did what she was told.

She got out the car and walked over to the door. She kissed the baby's forehead then sat the car seat down. She climbed back into the car, trying her hardest not to look back.

As soon as we drove off, she broke down. I looked over at Tiny to make sure she wasn't getting soft on a nigga. I understand life is a mother and how it could affect someone, but business was business, so this shit had to get done.

Barbie Scott
TRAP GYRL 3

Tiny…

No lie, I felt like I wanted to cry for her. I couldn't imagine having to leave one of my kids behind. But, I also understood in this game, it was kill or be killed. Dealing with all the madness with the whole Mike thing taught me that. That nigga was a real fuck boy by nature. Nobody gave a fuck about me or my kids, and not to mention, one of my best friends were dead behind the hands of the fucking Cartel.

Lately, me and Blaze had been catching body after body, but we couldn't get our hands on Mario. It was like the nigga was invisible. After watching my friend laid out in that Chapel, I wanted him, bad. I never thought the day would come that I would be out here on a killing spree with my Clyde.

Blaze and I had been doing great. We've been riding for each other since day one. I had one big secret and I didn't know how to tell him. I'm six weeks pregnant and I don't know how he would react to the news. He doesn't have any kids and I already birth three. To be honest, I didn't want another baby, especially not right now. It was too much going on in our lives for me to be tryna birth another baby.

We pulled up to the warehouse where Cash had instructed us to go. I had turned so cold hearted, I wanted to just body this bitch and get it over with. I was ready to get home, fuck my man, and eat up the entire house.

I looked over at Blaze and his big, chocolate ass was sexy as hell. I loved when he was in killer mode because he had this look as if he was so focused. Who would have ever thought we would be in love. Blaze was always so mean and quiet. Niya was so in love with him, but the nigga would never budge. The day we had sex in the trap was just a get back to Mike, and here we are now.

"Aye, ma, give me the keys," he walked up, knocking me out my thoughts.

I reached into my pockets to retrieve the keys to the Dungeon. The Dungeon was the cellar in the warehouse where we kept people until the killer came to put them out their misery.

Blaze escorted the woman down to the Dungeon, locked her in, and then came back out. He grabbed my hand and led me to the car.

"You know I love you, right?"

TRAP GYRL 3

"I know you do, ma," he replied. He then kissed me.

I don't know what this man was doing to me but he had me ready to marry his ass. I wanted that Cash & Nino type of love. I hated they were beefing, but I chose to stay out of it. She had called me and told me about her new little boo she had met and I was happy for her. I love Nino to death, but Cash was my best friend so her happiness was much more important.

"Let's go, baby girl," Blaze said, opening my car door. It was time we headed home and gave each other our loving.

I looked over at him and it looked like he was in deep thought. I had so much on my mind, I chose to just focus my attention on the night air.

"What's up, ma. Something on your mind?" he asked, looking from the highway to me, back to the highway.

"It's so much on my mind, really." I sighed, then looked back out my window. "Have you ever thought about leaving the game, Blaze?" I asked, but not once looking in his direction.

"Honestly, baby girl. Yes, I've thought about it, but shit, this all I know. Ms. Lopez and Cash had been so good to a nigga, shit, I don't want to just leave them."

"That's understandable, especially in a time like this. But, one day, you're gonna have to get out. I mean, we good with the money. We got an eight-bedroom home that's paid for and we could open some sort of business."

"Where is this coming from, Tee?" he said, calling me by my little nickname he gave me.

"I don't know, bae."

"Does it have something to do with you being pregnant?" he asked, with a smirk on his face.

How the fuck did he know? I thought to myself.

"What, you thought I didn't know?" he said, and I simply nodded my head.

"A nigga has been feeling sick lately. Not to mention, yo ass done got thicker and you think I haven't been paying attention to you eating like one of those African kids," he chuckled and grabbed my hand.

"So, now what?" I asked, unsure of how he was feeling.

"I mean, shit, it's up to you. I wouldn't mind having a shorty with you, but real shit, ma. I already got three, shit," he laughed, referring to my kids. That shit made my heart melt.

TRAP GYRL 3

"So, I guess we gotta handle this then?"

"It's all up to you, baby." He reached over and kissed me. There was nothing else to discuss.

Chapter X

Cash

I had walked into Trap Gyrl and there were dozens of flowers everywhere. At first, I thought they could have come from Brooklyn until I pulled the card off and began to read. I walked over to the first vase and began sniffing them. They were so refreshing. Jah was the perfect gentleman and I actually enjoyed his company. He was so sweet with a thuggish mentality just how I liked them. He texted me every day just to ask how was my day going. He made sure to text me every night just to say good night. He always sent me his new music, he even tried to get me into the music game.

I never told Jah what I did for a living, so he was left puzzled. I just prayed he'd never talk to someone that knew me because I knew they would tell it all. It was actually cool to have someone in a different field, other than the drug game. For once

TRAP GYRL 3

in my life, I felt normal and like a real human being. Jah was like that fresh breath of air that gave me life. As much as I wanted to take things further, I couldn't, because I didn't want him to get hurt. With the life I lived, he could end up dead and wouldn't even know why. Between the Cartel's, Brooklyn, and even Que's crazy ass, I didn't want to put him in a dangerous situation.

"So, I take it you like the flowers?" a masculine voice spoke from behind me.

I slowly turned around, with a huge grin and watched as Jah stood before me. We were so caught up in each other's gaze that either of us said one word. Every time we were together, there was an awkward silence between us as if we were trying hard to study each other.

"Yes, I do, thank you." I gave him a hug and pulled him towards my office.

On our way, walking towards my safe haven, Nikki and a few of the ladies were smiling ear to ear. I knew the minute we closed the door, the chatter would begin. Everybody and they mama knew Brook and I were split up but seeing this new man was a shock to everyone.

"You know, it's crazy I have actually been here a few times. A chick named Mo cut my hair," he said, taking a seat on my two-seater sofa. Just the mention of Monique's name almost caused me to go haywire. That bitch got around, I mean damn, what nigga in the city of Miami hadn't she smashed.

"Have yall ever?" I asked with a hand motion, referring to fucking.

"Nah, ma. That was my boy, Ryder's, little piece."

"Ryder? You knew him?"

"Yeah, that was my nigga."

Ryder was a little D-Boy that was heavy in the game. He copped his work from me and not to mention, he was fine as hell, but I never took it there with him.

"Damn, that shit sad," I said, shaking my head, thinking about my boy.

"Yeah, man. He offed himself over that chick, Raine."

"Yeah, he must have been in love. You know, I had met her a couple of times. Cute, young girl. I heard she killed herself, and then six months, later he killed himself."

"Yeah, that was fucked up."

"I miss my nig..." Jah went to say, but he was cut off by the sound of the door opening.

Barbie Scott
TRAP GYRL 3

When I looked away from Jah, Brook was standing at the door with a look of disgust. He looked pissed the fuck off. He made his way further into my office.

"Who this nigga?" He looked from Jah, and then back to me.

"Don't worry bout it, nigga. And, why are you here?" I asked, mad.

"Man, don't try and front a nigga, Cash. Who the fuck is this nigga.?" Brook said, then reached into his waistline for his strap.

I quickly ran from around my desk and jumped in between the two. Jah was now standing to his feet and was mugging Brook something serious.

"Nino, not here."

"Oh, I'm *Nino* now?"

"Look, we are not together so the company I keep around me is not your concern. But, since you wanna know, this is Jah, and yes, we're dating."

The moment I said it, Brook clenched his jaw. Jah wasn't backing down and that shit turned me on even more. Brook gave me one last look then walked out, upset. Right when the door shut, Nikki stuck her head in the door. I gave her a reassuring look, letting her know everything was ok, and she continued on about her day.

"I'm sorry, Jah. That's…" he cut me off.

"That's your child's father. I already know, future. But, tell me this, you still fucking him and don't lie to me, ma?' he asked like he was an urgency to know.

"No, I'm not."

"Ok, good. A nigga not in the position to be beefing over a woman when she still secretly seeing the next nigga. He busting up in here brandishing guns but he don't know me from a can of paint, Cash," Jah said, and lifted his shirt, exposing two guns on each side of his waistband. "I'm just not the type of nigga to disrespect a woman. I know that's your son's pops, and not to mention, this is your place of business."

"You have nothing to worry about," I said, then walked up to Jah and placed a kiss on his soft plump lips. From what he just said, only made me respect him that much more.

***

After I left Trap Gyrl, I was heading up to Juice to meet Jah. He wanted to have drinks, after everything that happened with Brooklyn. Jah was really growing on me. Everything about him was very intriguing. I didn't want to seem like a thot, but I was ready to break him off some of this good-good. It had been a minute since I had some dick, and my honey box was crying. I thought about taking him to my house but I didn't want Brook to pop up and all hell breaks loose. He swore he didn't have a wife at home so I would for sure see when I asked him to take me to his house.

The sound of my phone snapped me out of my thoughts. I really didn't want to answer because I didn't need any distractions. Once I saw it was Rosa, I quickly answered.

"Hey, Rosa."

"Cash, el bebe, he's missing," Rosa spoke in her native accent. She was crying, uncontrollably, to where I could barely understand a word.

"What do you mean, Rosa?"

"BJ. BJ, he's gone." She was still crying.

"Where did he go?" I shouted.

"I don't know, mija. His bedroom window was open, and now, he's missing."

I made a sudden stop on my brakes that caused my car to jerk. My phone fell to the floor and I couldn't even stop my tears.

Oh my God, my baby! I cried, slamming my hands against my steering wheel.

Barbie Scott
TRAP GYRL 3

After I gathered myself, I retrieved my phone that had fallen under my gas pedal. My hands were shaking, badly, and I could hardly dial the number. Just the thought of what these muthafuckas would do to my baby had me ready to tear up the entire state of Florida. I wanted to call my mother but I thought against it. I quickly made a U-Turn and went to the only person I knew I could confide in.

When I pulled up to the home, I was let in by the guards. I took my time getting out of the car because I didn't know what to say. How was I gonna break the news about BJ being kidnapped? What would I say? My son was kidnapped because his mother was on her way to get some dick. Just the thought broke me down, more.

I exit the car and finally made my way to the door. I rung the bell and waited patiently. After about five minutes, he answered the door, wearing a wife beater and some b-ball shorts. His eyes looked pleading and I knew the moment I told him what was going on, he would be on the same page as me. I couldn't even take it anymore. I fell into his arms with tears streaming down my face.

"They got him, Brook. Oh, my God, they got my baby," I cried.

"Who got him, Cash?"

Barbie Scott
TRAP GYRL 3

"I don't know. He was kidnapped. It has to be the Cartel."

"Come here, ma. Stop crying."

"I'm so sorry, Brook. Please, forgive me. It's all my fault. I'm so sorry," I cried into his arms.

He kissed the top of my forehead and pulled me to the couch. He cuddled me into his arm and rubbed my head, continuously.

Right when I was about to speak, I could have sworn I heard the sound of a baby crying. I lifted up from laying on Brook and eyed him, suspiciously. He wore a dumbfounded look that I knew all too well. I darted from my seat, up the stairs, towards his room. He was hot on my heels but I was determined to see what this nigga had going on.

I know this bitch, Tiffany, and her baby not staying here. I swear, I'ma kill him and this bitch, I thought, making it to his bedroom door.

I swung the door open ready to pounce on the bitch and I was shocked beyond words. I looked at Brook, who was now standing in the doorway. I walked over to the bed and picked up BJ. I kissed him over and over then sat him back down. I walked over to Brook and in one swift move, I whacked his ass across the face. I knew I was

TRAP GYRL 3

playing with fire but how the fuck could he work my blood like this?

He grabbed my hands and forcefully pushed me to the ground. I tried to jump up but he came down to the floor and landed right on top of me. With all my might, I struggled for him to get off me but he was too strong. He began kissing me so passionately, I could tell he missed every ounce of me. I was now caught up between anger and passion, but I couldn't help it. I kissed him back.

Chapter XI

Brooklyn Nino

I know what I did was petty as fuck, but I don't give two fucks. Damn right, I kidnapped my son because I needed a reason to get her to my crib. After I saw her and that nigga in Trap Gyrl, I was ready to body both their ass, right then and there. I sucked it up like the G I was and came up with another plan; kidnap my son. I called Ms. Lopez and she said Cash wasn't there. I hit Nikki and she was gone from the shop so I knew her ass had to be with that fuck nigga. Ms. Lopez, and Pedro knew I had BJ, and that's why they weren't blowing up our phones. I was sure, by now, they had told Ms. Rosa and that was the reason she had stopped blowing up Cash's phone. I guess my little stunt worked because I had her ass right where I wanted her.

When she slapped me, it kinda turned a nigga on. I knew she was mad because of BJ, so I let her

105

TRAP GYRL 3

have that. Once I kissed her and she didn't resist, I pressed my luck and took it further. I pulled her blouse over her head, forcefully. Next, I went down to her pants. Right now, I couldn't take things slow and be passionate with Cash because I needed to get this shit done before she changed her mind. Once I got her jeans down and pulled out of one pants leg, I dove straight into her love box, head first.

Her shit was dripping wet, and I wouldn't leave not one drop behind. I sucked, slurped, licked every piece of her pussy. The moment her head fell back, I knew there was no stopping. I made her ass bust two organisms then I came up for air. I stepped out my basketball shorts and looked into her lust filled eyes.

"You fucked that nigga, Cash?" I asked and prayed she would be truthful.

She looked at me with so much fire in her eyes before speaking. "No, but I was on my way to before Rosa called about BJ," she smirked.

Instead of me getting mad, I was just gonna take it out on her pussy. I forcefully slid every inch into her warm opening. Fuck taking my time, I rammed up into her with long hard strokes.

Damn, her pussy tight as a muthafucka, I thought as I bit my bottom lip. I started hitting her ass with death strokes and her eyes began to roll to the back of her head.

"So, you were gonna give my pussy up?" I pounded into her pussy. Her mouth was open but no words were coming out so I thrust harder.

"Ooh, shit, Brook. Uhhh, I'm about to cum!" she was finally able to speak.

"So, you were about to give my pussy up?"

"No, daddy, I wasn't. Oh my, I love you! I love you!" she shouted out and I could feel her body shake, which let me know she was cumming.

The moisture of her pussy made me cum right along with her. Little did she know, I wasn't done with her ass.

After we caught our breaths, we lifted off the floor. When we walked to the bed, BJ was knocked out sleep. Cash looked at him, then me. She shook her head and walked off towards the restroom. I hesitated for a moment before following her. When I walked in, she was in the shower. I wanted to hop in with her, but when I saw her tears following, I went and took a seat on the bed. I really wanted to console Cash, but I knew why she was crying; my deceitful bullshit.

TRAP GYRL 3

Once she got out the shower, I watched her as she dried her hair. Her eyes were bloodshot red and that shit made me feel worse.

"Come here, ma." I grabbed her arm and guided her to the bed. I really didn't know what to say but I was gonna try my hand.

"I'm sorry, ma." I shook my head. "I'm sorry for everything. If you just give a nigga a chance to make it up to you, I promise on my mother's grave, I'ma make it right."

Everything I said was the God to honest truth. She looked like she was contemplating on what she wanted to say. The look on her face let me know it wasn't gonna be good.

"Look, Brook, I'm not gonna lie nor pretend like I'm not hurt because I'm beyond hurt. I love you more than life itself and I've realized that since we've been apart. Yes, I want my family back, but I don't think I can deal with you running to that bitch Tiffany."

She just used me for my dick, I thought to myself as I watched her mouth move. It was like I had zoned out and the only thing I heard was jibber jabber. I was quickly snapped out my thoughts because the sound of her phone ringing.

"Hello." She answered on the second ring.

TRAP GYRL 3

"Oh, yeah?" she said with a smile on her face. I couldn't hear what the caller was saying but I could tell by the look on Cash's face it was quite interesting.

"I'm on my way," were her last words before hanging up. She looked at me then quickly turned and began putting her clothes on.

"I'm sorry, Brook, I have to go. Something came up at the warehouse."

"I'm going with you!" I jumped to my feet and began to dress.

"And, just what are we gonna do with your son that you kidnapped?" she smirked, and I couldn't help but laugh.

"Sorry bout that, ma."

"Yeah, I admit, that was a good one. But I'm ok, Brook. Plus, I wanted him to spend the night with you," she hit me with. That shit cut like a knife. I was more than sure after I hit her with this dope dick, I would be up in it for the rest of the night but she fooled the hell out of me.

I just shook my head and went and laid in my spot on the bed, next to BJ. She looked at me one last time before walking out of the door.

Cash...

I was burning rubber trying to get to the warehouse. As bad as I wanted to talk to Brook, that call from Blaze fucked up my entire train of thought. I really wanted to lay everything on the line about how I felt. I couldn't believe I gave in, especially with the little stunt he pulled with BJ. At first, it felt like he was damn near raping me, and that shit turned me on more. Seeing him in that wife beater and the dick print in those shorts had me feeling some type of way. The problem with

Brook was he thought that sex could fix the way I felt, when in fact, it didn't do anything. Yes, I wanted him just as bad as he wanted me but the fact still remained, he had someone other than me he would have to cater to. I couldn't see myself sitting at home and him going to see his baby.

When I went into the restroom, his phone was on the sink. I quickly slid it open and it was on Tiffany's Instagram. There was a picture of her holding her baby in the hospital. It was like she had just had him but there was not one pic of Brook. In all honesty, I don't think I would ever trust him around her so I was not about to stress myself out. I guess we could smash from time to time, but right now, I was gonna do me.

When I pulled up into the warehouse parking lot, Blaze's car was the only one there. I swerved my car around to the back and walked inside to handle my business. When I walked in, Blaze was leaned up against the table and Tiny was sitting in the chair in front of him. I looked her up and down because something looked strange about her. It was like she had a glow.

This bitch is pregnant, I thought to myself before approaching the two.

"Where is she?" I asked.

With a simple head nod, he pointed down to the dungeon.

When I made it downstairs, it was kind of dark. The only light that shined into the room was the glare from the streetlight shining through the tiny window above. She was tied up to a piece of metal like she was Jesus getting ready to die on the cross for our sins. She was far from Jesus but the bitch was surely about to be punished.

I used the barrel of my gun to lift her chin. When she looked at me, her eyes grew wide as saucers. I stared at her with a menacing stare before uttering one word.

"Well, hello, Stephanie," I smirked.

"Just get it over with, bitch," she said and dropped her head.

My first thought was to torture the bitch, but I didn't have time to chastise her, so I was gonna give her that wish. I raised my gun and fired two shots into her head, and then two more shots into her chest. She died, instantly. I hated I had to be so raw but this bitch had to go. There was no point in calling Mario or holding her ransom because my dad had already told me Mario had cut her off.

I walked back upstairs and Blaze and Tiny were still in the same spot.

"Just burn this bitch down, Blaze," I said and walked towards the door.

Before I made it completely out, I turned to face Tiny.

"Let me know what color bassinet you want," I hit her with a smirk and walked out to my car.

Chapter XII

Breelah

I had just taken my medicine because I was in so much pain. All I wanted to do was rest because I was extremely tired. It had been a couple of weeks since the incident with Cash and Que. No lie, that shit hurt me, bad. I mean, I had heard about their prior relationship, but damn, I thought since she had gotten with my brother, her and Que would have dead that shit.

I had finally talked to Brook and he told me what happened at the wedding and everything with Tiffany. I can't say that I don't blame her for wanting to get back at Brook, but damn, did anyone think about me and my feelings? As bad as I wanted to tell my brother, I didn't even bother. I wanted him to know but I didn't want him hurt as well. Everything in the dark would eventually come to the light, just like that call I had gotten about Que, on our way to the wedding. And, not to mention, who had shot me. I wanted to tell Brooklyn everything because he was the one that I could confide in.

Me and Bronx were pretty close, but me and Brooklyn were closer. Brook had basically raised me after my parents were murdered. He paid for me to go to college, he bought my car, and even the three-bedroom house I was living in that's in Miami. He kept the rent paid while I was in school and even purchased me a condo near campus. Brooklyn had basically stepped up to the father role so I felt I owed him my life. I'm happy to be alive because every time I heard his voice when I was in the coma, it broke my heart. My brother's world would have been shattered if something had gone wrong.

The sound of tiny pebbles hitting my window brought me out of my daydream. I lifted off my bed and slowly walked to the window. When I looked out, Que was standing at the bottom, looking up at me with pleading eyes. I watched him for a moment, not saying a word.

"Can I holla at you?" he shouted.

Without a word, I shook my head and went to unlock the door.

Barbie Scott
TRAP GYRL 3

When I let him inside, he walked straight to my room. He had been texting and calling me every day but every call went unanswered. I finally closed the door and followed him into my room. When I walked in, he was sitting at the foot of my bed with his head down. I walked over to the head of my bed and laid back on my pillow that I had propped up.

"I'm sorry, baby girl," he said, turning around to face me. "I know I fucked up, but I wanna fix this shit."

"And, how do you figure you could do that? I mean, come on, Quintin, I walked in on you with your fucking face buried in my sister in law's pussy. So, please tell me how could you fix it?"

"I know I was wrong, Bree. It was like a spare of the moment thing. A nigga been so stressed out with everything that's been going on. Cash came to me crying about some shit with Nino. I was already upset about some shit with my BM, so I took advantage of the situation. I was so torn up that I forgot about you and your feelings. So again, I'm sorry."

"Y'all thought I was dead!" I spoke with a now tear stained face.

He ran over to me and began to console me.

TRAP GYRL 3

"Look, ma, I'ma be real with you. I didn't fuck her and hadn't fucked her since her and Nino been rocking. If this shit costing me to lose you, I swear, it would never happen again. I made some foolish decisions in my life, living reckless, fucking with different bitches, but I swear ain't nobody worth me losing you."

"Not even, Cash?" I asked, truthfully.

He looked at me sincerely and spoke the words I wanted to hear.

"Not even Cash, baby girl." He looked me dead in my eyes.

I got quiet and focused in on the TV as if I were watching it. In actuality, it was watching me because I was in such a deep thought.

"They took Qui from me," he said, breaking me from my thoughts.

"Who took Qui?"

"DCFS. She had swallowed some dope, thanks to her crackhead mama." He shook his head, repeatedly.

The moment he said they took Qui, my heart went out to him. I grabbed his hand and he took it as an invitation because he laid his head on the good side of my shoulder. He looked so hurt and it made me give in. I still had questions, I needed answers, but for now, I would let them go until I talked to Brooklyn for insurance.

***

The next morning, I woke up bright and early due to the sharp pains that were shooting through my body. Que was inside the restroom, on the phone. I lifted out my bed to retrieve my medicine from the cabinet. When I walked in, he looked at me with a slight smile. He swatted me on my ass as I walked over to retrieve the Rite Aid pharmacy bag.

"Good morning, baby girl."

"Morning." I smiled weakly.

"What you got up today?" he asked, walking back into my room.

"Just an online class then I need to go speak with someone."

"Someone? Someone, like who?"

"Dang, you nosey, nigga." I giggled and headed out the room towards the kitchen. He was hot on my tracks.

"It bet not be a nigga, Bree," he had the nerve to say.

"Boy, I ain't thinking about no niggas."

TRAP GYRL 3

"Okay, good. Because I'll still fuck you up. Bullet wombs and all, ma."

We both laughed.

"Nah, but for real. I'm bout to head home and pack a bag. I gotta run to the trap and pick up some bread from Blaze, then I'ma be back, alright?"

"Okay, I should be back by then."

"A'ight," he said, right before he kissed me.

Once I was finish getting dressed, I headed outside to my ride and climbed in. As bad as I didn't want to take this trip, I needed answers so I had to suck it up.

After the thirty-minute drive, I pulled up. I was let into the gate by the security and made my way to the door. After a few minutes, the door finally opened.

"Hi, Ms. Lopez, Is Cash home?"

"Breelah!" she shouted, happy to see me. She pulled me in for a hug then told me Cash was upstairs, waiting for BJ to get home.

After talking with Ms. Lopez for a bit, I made my way up the spiral stairs and headed to Cash's room. I knocked twice before she told me to come in.

"Hey, Bree," she said like she was also happy to see me. There was no doubt in my mind Cash

TRAP GYRL 3

was excited by my presence. Despite what went on with her and Que, I knew she genuinely loved me.

I took a seat on the lounge chair and I waited for her to talk. She was the one that got caught up so I felt she was the one that should speak up first. After the awkward silence, she finally began...

"Look, Bree, I just wanna start off by saying I'm sorry. I never meant to hurt you and you know that. I love you like a little sister and I don't want anything to interfere with that. I had just found out that your brother slept with Arcelie, someone who worked for me and my mother. Not to mention, the whole thing with the Tiffany situation. I guess I was just out to hurt Brook but I didn't think to worry about you and your feelings. I hate that you had to see Que between my legs but what I could ensure you is that we didn't have sex."

"So basically, he just gave you head."

"That's it, that's all. I'm not saying it was right, but I am saying I really apologize and I promise it won't happen again. Que really loves you. I've never seen him act like this over a woman."

"Except for you," I smirked at her, she began giggling.

"Except for me, little lady."

Barbie Scott
TRAP GYRL 3

Right when I was gonna ask her about the situation with Que and Bronx, Nino walked in with my nephew in his arms. Cash and I both looked up at him because we were unsure of how much he had heard. When he walked over and kissed Cash's cheek, we sighed in relief.

I pulled BJ out of his arms and began playing with his cute self. It was crazy that he looked so much like Brooklyn, except with Cash's big round eyes. His head was full of huge jet black curls and he had an Indian brown complexion that I was sure came because of Cash's genes. I tossed him in the air and he immediately began to laugh. Playing with BJ made me wonder how would my life be if I had kids. Especially if it was Que's baby. His daughter was so pretty that I knew with our genes combined, we would also make a beautiful baby.

I took BJ downstairs so we could go find Ms. Lopez and talk her ear off. I wanted to leave Brook and Cash alone because I knew they were having problems.

Chapter XIII

Brooklyn Nino

Driving down Martin Luther King Hwy, I was in a zone. I was bumping a song called "Milk Mike" By a rapper chick from Cali named Barbie Amor. Cash had put me up on her a while ago and even mentioned she wanted to fly her to Miami to perform. The more I listen to the song, I felt heartache. I was Cash's Milk Mike. The way she held me down, I knew couldn't no other bitch step to the plate. We got money together, bodied shit together, and not a soul could come between what we had. I couldn't believe Cash had actually stepped out on me with this nigga, though. I had to get her mind off him and make sure she didn't give him what belonged to me.

When I dropped off BJ, I was by her bedroom door, the entire time, listening to her and Breelah talk. I heard everything. When I say I was crushed, I

121

Barbie Scott
TRAP GYRL 3

was broken. Even though Que had only given her some head, they still doubled back on something they both acted like was over. I knew Que would always love Cash but I never thought she would give in to him. I also know that shit was a major get back, on her behalf, from all the fucked up shit I had done.

The day she left me and BJ sleep in her house, I had picked up my phone and saw that she had read my text. Then, I got a call that she beat Arcelie's ass at her shop, over me, and that shit really crushed me. I knew I had known baby girl from somewhere, I just couldn't put my finger on it. I guess that's what I get for thinking with my dick. All the shit I put Cash through, I was now regretting. I could tell she wanted to give us another try, but the shit with Tiffany was eating her up. I needed to get my family back so I had to do what I had to do.

Tiffany ended up having a boy. The DNA said that I was indeed 99.9 percent the father. I loved my son to death, but no lie, I prayed every day that he wouldn't be mine. Braylen Carter, six pounds and four ounces. Tiffany gave birth to him at only eight months, but because he weighed so much, they let him come right home.

Barbie Scott
TRAP GYRL 3

When I pulled up Tiffany's house, I walked in
and went straight to my son's room like I always
did. Tiffany thought, once the baby came, we were
gonna play house but that shit wasn't happening.
On a few occasions, she tried giving me some
pussy, but the bitch couldn't even suck my dick. It
had been a while since I had some pussy. I had cut
Arcelie off that last day she left my house. It was
something fishy with that bitch to begin with. I
should have known something was up because she
knew shit that I never told her, like my name being
Brooklyn, when in fact, I told her Nino.

"Hey, baby daddy," Tiffany said, interrupting
me from my thoughts.

I just looked at her with so much disgust.

"Where's my son?"

"Damn, that's all you worry about."

I shot her a look with so much hatred that she
just shut the fuck up with the quickness.

"What else am I supposed to worry about? Sure
not you, ma. I told you from the gate, we wasn't
about to play house."

I walked out of her bedroom and went to
Braylen's room. I was tired and needed to take a
nap. When I walked in, he was sound asleep in his
crib so I climbed into the twin sized bed that was in

TRAP GYRL 3

his room and just fucked around on my phone until
I dozed off.

***

    I opened my eyes and had to recollect myself. I
looked around the room and when I saw the Noah's
ark paintings, I knew I was still in Braylen's room. I
got up and walked over to his crib and his eyes were
wide open. I picked him up and cuffed him into my
arms. I then walked into Tiffany's room and she was
laying on her bed, knocked out. I quickly went into
my son's room and began packing his diaper bag.
Once I was done, I sat him snuggled into his car
seat and sat his bag down beside him.

    I walked back into Tiffany's room and she was
still laying in the same position. I stood at the door
and watched her as she slept. When I gathered my
thoughts, I walked over to the bed and grabbed the
pillow that was on the side of her. With both hands
and all the strength I had, I put it over her face. She
woke up and grabbed my arm, but it was too late.
Her eyes were bulging out of her sockets as she
struggled to scream. The pillow over her face
muffled out her cries. I tried my hardest to suffocate
her and when I finally felt her arms fall, I knew she

TRAP GYRL 3

was out. I took my gun from my waist and put two bullets into her head. Once I saw that she wasn't coming back, I walked into the kitchen and busted the window and left the door ajar so it would look like a break in. I walked back into the living room and grabbed my baby, and then headed for my car.

I hated what I had done to Tiff because my son had to grow up without his mother. But, I needed my family back, and if this is what had to be done for me to get them, then so be it. I knew if I kept Tiffany around, my relationship with Cash would never be the same. There was no woman on earth I loved more than Cash, other than Bree, so by any means, we would live happily ever after. Once we killed Mario, I was gonna take Cash on a cruise and have us a private wedding in the Bahamas. One way or the other, I was going to marry the love of my life.

When I pulled up to her house, the gate opened and I pulled in. I parked my car at the entrance of the door, just in case she tried to fight me, then I could just run out, hop in my shit, and bounce. I knew that showing up with Braylen would kill her but she had to get over it because she would be coming home and Braylen would be permanently living with us.

Barbie Scott
TRAP GYRL 3

I rang the doorbell three times and waited patiently for her to answer. I knew, normally around this time, Ms. Lopez would be at Esco's so I would be meeting face to face with my wife. After a few moments, she swung the door open.

She crossed her arms over one another, shifted all her weight to one side, and gave me a look that said, "Boy, you got me twisted." She looked from me to the car seat and then back to me. I guess my eyes cried out to her because her face had finally softened.

Chapter XIV

Que

Bree and I had being doing a lot better over these last few days. I catered to her in every way possible. I needed her to forgive a nigga and believe me when I said that I was sorry. I really loved baby girl and I really felt bad about her catching us. I promised Bree it would never happen again, and I was more than sure of it because I knew Cash wouldn't let it happen again. Yes, I lied and told Bree *not even Cash,* because everybody and they granny knew that if Cash gave me that opportunity again, I would bust that pussy all the way open. Indeed, I was falling for Bree, but the fact of the matter is, she wasn't Cash. Cash was really cut from a different kind of cloth. Not only is she sexy, rich, and got ass for days, but she has a good ass heart, a dope personality and she's the true definition of a rider. She held me down, with or without us

127

fucking. Even if I had a bitch, she would still step up to the plate.

"You good?" Breelah asked, pulling me from a hella daze. She clenched my hand tighter and looked at me with a worried look.

"Yeah, I'm straight, ma." I sighed, knowing damn well I wasn't.

We had just left the facility visiting Qui. I knew it would be hard but I had to see my baby girl. What really broke me down was when she cried because I handed her back to the lady who ran the unit Qui was in. As of now, I was getting weekly visits and was instructed to take a few parenting classes, and then I could get full custody. Diane informed me, I had a good chance because Qui wasn't in my care when it happened, however, they would question my criminal history. The part that shocked me was Breelah mentioned her getting custody if necessary, and that shit made me love shawty even more.

It was like this bitch Keisha had vanished into thin air. She knew what was best for her because I have killed people over smaller shit. I just hoped she would hear about another woman stepping up to the plate to raise her child.

Barbie Scott
TRAP GYRL 3

"Baby, answer yo phone," Bree said, grabbing my phone from the cup holder. I was so lost in my thoughts, I didn't even hear that shit ringing.

When I looked at the caller ID, it was a weird ass number. I answered, hesitantly.

"Yeah!"

"Que, Que, Que," the voice spoke in a heavy accent.

I looked at the phone in disbelief because that voice only belonged to one person.

"First, you fuck my daughter and then you kill her?" he spoke and then paused.

Fuck this nigga talking 'bout?

"Who is it, bae?" Bree asked, but I didn't even respond.

"You just keep disappointing me, my man. I've been letting you slide with you fucking up a hit on Carter, but my daughter, I can't let that slide. Now I know you didn't kill Stephanie because you can't seem to do anything right. But, I know those fucking Lopez's had something to do with it. I'm telling you one time, I want bloodshed and if you don't, I'm gonna kill everybody around you, starting with that precious girlfriend of yours. Breelah Carter, am I right?" he said, but I remained quiet.

Barbie Scott
TRAP GYRL 3

Breelah was grilling me so I tried to remain as calm as possible. What tripped me out was him saying Stephanie was dead. And, he was right, that had Cash writing all over it.

"Bloodshed, Quintin!" he said, calling me by my fucking government. Again, I didn't respond.

He hung up.

"Que, is everything ok?" Breelah asked, sounding concerned. Of course, I couldn't tell her it was Mario so I thought of the first lie.

"It was a recording from the women's jail. My baby mama locked up."

"Damn," was all she said, shaking her head. I left it at that.

Instead of going home, I pulled up to a restaurant on Bay Shore. I needed to clear my mind from Qui because the moment I left her, I missed her little butt. Fuck what that nigga Mario was talking about. Yeah, I knew he would definitely come after me, but shit, I was already a dead man walking. It was weird how he had the nerve to talk shit about any killings when it was his fault I was walking around with a bandaged fucking torso now.

Once the valet took the keys to the whip, a hostess walked me and Bree inside to an empty table. We placed an order for two bottles of Belaire

champagne and some chilled oysters as an
appetizer. Looking at Bree, her ass was so sexy. She
was rocking some jeans and a blazer with a top that
was displaying her nice plump titties. Just looking
at her had my dick hard. The smile that crept across
her face made me smile but the look in her eyes told
that she had a lot on her mind. Something was
bothering baby girl, heavy, but she failed to mention
anything.

The waiter walked back over with our drinks
and appetizer and began taking our order. The
minute she walked off, I slid into the booth on the
side of Bree. I made her turn around and I traced her
titties with soft wet kisses. She began giggling,
which made me go further.

"You should have worn a dress, ma," I laughed
and it made her giggle harder.

"Stop, nasty," she said, but the slight moan that
escaped her lips told me she didn't want me to stop.

"Breelah."

We both turned around at the sound of
someone calling her name. When I looked up, it
was a tall, light skin nigga that wore his head in two
braids. I looked from him to her, and she wore a
look of shock.

"Ismel?" she smiled, looking at ol boy.

TRAP GYRL 3

"How you been, ma?" he asked, not looking at me, once.

"I've been good, how you been doing?"

"I've been smooth. A nigga miss you, though," he had the nerve to say, as if I wasn't sitting there.

A sense of nervousness took over Bree because she began fidgeting in her seat.

I jumped to my feet and mugged the nigga. He had me all the way fucked up.

"I'll advise you to get the fuck on, my nigga."

"So, you got niggas speaking for you now?" he asked, looking at Bree.

"No, please, Qu..."

Before she could finish, it was already too late. I hit the nigga so hard in his nose, it sounded like it broke, on impact. He fell back into the next table, and then quickly jumped to his feet. He must have read the look on my face because he didn't bother to swing back. He looked at Bree, who had her head down, and then back at me.

"I'll be seeing you around, homie," he said and walked off.

"Nigga, I'll see you outside," I said, ready to follow behind him.

By this time, the entire restaurant was watching us. Breelah jumped to her feet and grabbed my arm.

Barbie Scott
TRAP GYRL 3

My first instinct was to yank from her but the look
in her eyes was pleading. I took my seat and grilled
her ass.

"Who the fuck was that, Bree?"

"That was umm… It was my ex."

"Yo' ex, huh?"

"Yes, Que. I haven't seen him since I've been
back from school."

"So, y'all went to school together?"

"Yes," she said, just above a whisper. "But he
graduated before me."

"You fucked that nigga?" I asked. I already
knew the answer, but I still wanted to hear it from
her.

She shook her head, yes, and I don't know why,
but that shit pissed me off more than I was before. I
know he was before me, but just the thought of
another nigga having his way with her wasn't sitting
well with me.

"He was my first, Que."

"So, what the fuck that mean?"

"It means, I fucked him before I even knew
you. I'll dare you sit here and try to bar me when
you ain't no fucking saint," she said, sounding mad,
but I didn't give a fuck.

TRAP GYRL 3

The waiter walked up with our food and sat it down in front of us. I was still so mad, I had lost my appetite. I pushed the plate from in front of me and looked out the window. I could feel her eyes burning a hole through me so I kept my head straight to show her ass I was by far, bothered.

"Look, if you gonna act like this, we could just go," she said, but I still didn't look her way.

I stood from my seat, walked towards the door, and headed out the restaurant.

I stood there and waited about ten minutes for the valet driver to bring the car around, but Bree's ass never came out.

Once the car pulled up, I climbed in and patiently waited. After another ten minutes, she finally brought her ass out. She had her phone to her ear and had the nerve to walk past my car. At first, I wasn't about to bite into her little game but when I saw she was serious, I jumped out my ride. I tossed another twenty to the valet and told him to park the car again. I jogged in the direction I saw her walking, but her ass was kind of far.

"Breelah!" I called her name, but she kept walking.

I shook my head at her stubborn ass and ran a little faster. When I finally caught up to her, she was

TRAP GYRL 3

halfway by the water. I let her ass walk all the way because I had something for her. I ran up to her and dove on her ass, making her fall into the sandy bit of ocean.

"Que, my hair!" she whined like the brat she was.

"I don't give a fuck. Look at my shoes. These some brand-new Jay's, girl."

"Fuck yo Jay's," she laughed like the shit was funny.

"Oh, fuck my Jay's?"

I dipped her fresh press right into the water, soaking it, completely.

"Que!" she was shouting but rubbing her face at the same time, trying to get the salted water from out of her eyes.

We began wrestling in the water, both of us were laughing. My mission was complete. I, for once, had her smiling. I rolled her ass off me and pinned her down into the sand. We were at the beginning of the oceans currents so the water only covered the bottom of her. I looked into her big ass eyes and it was like she was her soul was calling out to me.

"You're crazy, man." she said with a short sigh.

Barbie Scott
TRAP GYRL 3

"I'm crazy for you.," I said with my sincerest look.

I kissed her, and when she didn't resist, I kissed her harder and more passionate.

She better be lucky it's still a little sunny or I'll have her ass bent over, I thought to myself, admiring her pretty ass.

Chapter XV

Cash Lopez

"Why did you bring this baby here, Brooklyn?" I eyed him with a serious expression.

"It's a long story, Cash." He shook his head and walked over to the couch.

The baby began to cry so he pulled him out his car seat and safely held him over his shoulder. I couldn't see his face, but honestly, I didn't care to. I looked at him one last time, and right when I was about to head back upstairs, my mother and Esco came through the front door. Esco's eyes grew wide, however, my mother took it upon herself to run towards Brook and the baby.

"Mijo," my mother smiled, grabbing the baby from Brook's arms. She began talking to him in Spanish as she snuggled him close into her boobs.

I went upstairs to my room and snuggled up under my own damn baby. I examined him as he slept, peacefully. He had grown so much. He was

TRAP GYRL 3

long in length and his little-self was chubby as ever.
He was finally sitting up and trying to hold his
bottle on his own. I kissed his tiny cheek and
watched him as his stomach heaved up and down.

My son was precious.

Since he'd been here, I had thoughts about
getting fully out of the game. I even thought about
moving into my own crib so that I wouldn't be
around anything that had to do with drugs. I guess
that was a mother's love. Two things I knew for
sure, my mother would die if I moved out and she
was never leaving the game. Our house had too
many bedrooms and was very huge. In all honesty,
it was too damn big for only two people. I knew,
eventually, I would be moving back to Brook's, but
I would always come home and have my room
because I hated leaving my mother alone.
Sometimes, I often wondered why didn't she just
move with my dad because she spent most of her
days there.

"May I come in?" Brook asked, walking in
uninvited.

"Sure," I spoke, nonchalantly, then focused
back on my son.

He walked to the opposite side of the bed and
kneeled on his knees. He began rubbing BJ's hair. It

was like BJ sensed he was in his presence because he started moving in his sleep. I guess my mother still had Brook's son because he didn't have him in his arms. I looked at him and waited for some sort of explanation to why in the fuck would he bring that bitch's baby to my house.

"Pack you and BJ a bag, Cash," he spoke then stood to his feet.

I looked at him like he had lost his forever lasting mind.

"I'm not asking you, I'm telling." He walked out my room, slamming the door behind him.

This nigga got his fucking nerves, I thought as I lifted from my bed.

I didn't have any more fight in me, so I simply complied with his request.

Moving from my room to BJ's, I packed our bags, ready to be bothered with his crazy ass daddy. Once I was finished, I called out to Brook so he could help take the things downstairs. I walked back into my room and slipped BJ into his one-piece teddy romper.

"You ready?" Brook asked, walking back into my room.

I nodded yes and grabbed BJ off the bed.

TRAP GYRL 3

When we made it downstairs, my mother was sitting on the couch with that other baby nestled up in her arms.

"Cash, did you see the baby? he's so cute," my mother cooed.

"No, I didn't see him, mother," I snarled.

She and Brook both looked at me while Esco sat on the sideline, snickering. Ms. Rosa walked in, followed by Pedro, and she ran over to BJ, who was now cozy in his car seat.

"Bye, mi bebe," she smiled, rubbing the top of BJ's head. She then walked over to Brook and playfully punched him in his arm.

"Ouch!" he laughed, rubbing his arm. "What was that for?" he smirked, already knowing the answer.

"Brooklyn, you almost gave me a heart attack kidnapping mi bebe."

Everyone fell out laughing.

My mother found it very funny because she was dying of laughter.

"I'm sorry, Ms. Rosa, but I had to get Cash back, somehow. And, it worked," he smirked, looking in my direction.

Once we were ready to walk out the door, Pedro looked at me and said, "Cash, be safe."

Barbie Scott
TRAP GYRL 3

The look in his eyes told me exactly what he meant. He was referring to me killing Mario's daughter.

I gave him a look that confirmed I was indeed the one who pulled the trigger. I simply nodded my head and we walked out, heading for Brook's car.

I strapped BJ in, and he sat his baby's car seat beside BJ's. He closed the door and went to the driver seat, and I did the same. We jumped on the highway, heading for his mansion. I had so many thoughts running through my mind, I remained quiet.

Once we finally made it, I grabbed BJ out his seat and latched him over my shoulder.

"Cash, you didn't buckle Braylen in?" Brook asked.

"No! Nigga, that's your job." *What the fuck.* I walked off towards the house.

I gave him one quick glance and he was shaking his head.

Oh well. I kept it moving right into the house. I hope he didn't think because the baby was here, I was supposed to attend to him. Call me petty, but that wasn't my responsibility.

He better be lucky I even came.

Barbie Scott
TRAP GYRL 3

Once inside the house, I went upstairs to lay BJ
down in his bed he had in Brook's house. I got to
the room and was stopped in my tracks. There were
two baby beds set up. The room was decorated
nicely with blue skies and teddy bears. But, what
puzzled me was, why did my baby have to share
rooms with that other child?

When Brook walked in, I got dead in on his
ass.

"All the rooms in this house and my baby gotta
share rooms with him." I gave him an evil glare.
"It's just a way for them to bound, Cash."

"Well, he bonds with me just fine."

"Stop being petty, ma. This is my son and he's
a part of me, which makes him a part of you."

"Exactly! He's a part of you, which makes,
him, and not shit to me." I stormed towards his
room with BJ still in my arms.

"Why the fuck you gotta be so petty?" he
stormed in right behind me.

"Petty" Nigga, petty is you for showing up to
my fucking door with a baby that's not mine. Petty
is, you even asking me to come here with you and
your fucking baby. And, to make matter worst,
petty is, you making my fucking son share a room

TRAP GYRL 3

when its four other rooms here!" I shouted as tears
began to stream down my face.

I was beyond hurt, and I guess, I just showed it.
I couldn't hold it in anymore. Seeing him with a
child that he bared with another woman broke me
down. I couldn't even stop crying, as I began to rock
BJ and pace the room. The facial expression I wore
must have showed him I was hurt because his face
softened and he sat down on the bed. He looked at
me with pleading eyes but that shit didn't faze me. I
stormed out the room and went to the patio. This is
where I would be sitting, for the time being. I
needed to get my thoughts together.

***

The next morning, I woke up to the sound of a
baby crying. My motherly instinct kicked in, so I
quickly lifted up. For a moment, I thought I was
home, in my bed, until I looked around and realized
I was at Brook's house. I walked into the nursery
where Brook had taken BJ during the middle of the
night, because if it was up to me, my baby would be
sleeping in the bed with us. When I walked into the
nursery, BJ was still asleep. The other baby was
screaming at the top of his lungs, and that's exactly

where I left him. I stood at the top of the stairs, calling Brook's name but he never answered. I went back into the room to retrieve my phone and placed a call.

"Sup, lil mama?" he answered on the first ring.

I slightly smiled because I hadn't heard him call me that in a while.

"Where are you?" I tried to sound annoyed.

"I'm getting breakfast. What's up?"

"Okay. Well, your son is crying."

"Damn, Cash, give him a bottle or something."

"Once again, he is not my responsibility. Should I drop him off to his mama?" I asked, being sarcastic.

"Man, I'm on my way." He hung up.

I went back into the nursery and grabbed BJ before this little nigga woke him up. I took him into Brook's room and laid him in the bed. I laid beside him and began browsing through the television for something to watch. I tried turning the television up to drown out the sound of that baby's cries but it wasn't helping, which was annoying my soul.

"Boom!" Brook busted through the door with his crying ass baby in his arms. He grilled me before speaking.

TRAP GYRL 3

"You know that's fucked up you just let my baby cry, Cash. Stop being childish!"

"How about I just take my childish ass home!" I barked back. I got up to began grabbing my belongings.

"Bye!" was all he said, which hurt me to the utmost.

Exactly my point, I couldn't compare with a child. No matter what, that baby would always come first. To say I was beyond hurt, would be an understatement, I was crushed. I was so used to Brook putting me on a peddle stool. I was so used to me coming *second to none* in his life, and most of all, I was used to being his number one priority, but now, I had to come second. It was different coming second to my own child, but to be put on the back burner for another bitch's baby, a bitch who tried to ruin my wedding, a bitch who played the role of a side chick and was actually put into a position of having a piece of my husband; I was distraught.

After grabbing me and BJ's belongings, I headed down the stairs and making my way to the door. Brook was behind me but not saying one word. As bad as I wanted to cry, I just couldn't. I was tired of crying. Shit, crying hadn't really gotten me anywhere. I took one quick glance at Brook and his jaws were clenched tight. He showed no remorse, he simply let me go without a fight. I knew he was mad about how I acted with his son but I really didn't give a fuck. I needed time. He thought that I would be over this in one night, NOPE!

As soon as I grabbed the nob, I was stuck in my tracks. Looking through the glass windows, I saw the figure of two men in suits.

Detectives, I thought as I looked back at Brook.

The look I wore alerted him because he ran to the door and was also stopped in his tracks.

Chapter XVI

Brooklyn Nino

F uck they want? I thought as I walked to the door. Because of the slight tent, I knew they couldn't see us, but whatever they wanted, I chose to face the music. I slowly opened my door and looked between the two officers. I know my face showed anger but it had nothing to do with them. I was pissed off at Cash's immature ass. I know this was a bit much for her, but shit, this is my son so she had to accept it or get lost; straight up!

"Hi, I'm Officer Galda, and this is my partner, Officer Jacobs. Are you Brooklyn Carter, sir?"

"Yes," I nodded my head.

"May we come in to have a word with you?" Officer Galda asked.

I nodded my head and moved to the side to let them in. I gave Cash a mean mug before walking over to take a seat. She stood still with a worried look, but I ignored her and focused my attention on the pigs sitting in my living room.

147

Barbie Scott
TRAP GYRL 3

"Mr. Carter, we have some bad news." Officer Jacobs sighed, then looked me in the eyes.

I prayed everything was ok with Bronx because he was the only one living wild and free, at the moment.

"I'm sorry to tell you this, sir, but Ms. Tiffany Scott was found dead in her home this morning. It appeared to be a break-in and the neighbor found her with two bullet wombs to the head."

The moment he was done, I sat with my mouth open and heart on the floor. I shook my head and dropped it into the palm of my hands.

"When was the last time you spoke to Ms. Scott?"

"Well, the day she dropped my baby off to me."

The officer looked at me like he felt sorry for me, continuously shaking his head. He then stood to his feet, followed by the other officer.

"We have to get going but you take care, sir. Sorry for your lost," Officer Galda spoke, then headed out the door, followed by his partner.

Once they were out the home, with my back to the door, I leaned my head back and sighed in relief. When Cash and I locked eyes, she stared at me, curiously. It was like the entire time, she was trying to read me. I had to have given myself up because her look went from worried to a *you're crazy* look. She began shaking her head, but with a smirk.

The sound of Braylen crying made us both look up the stairs. I looked at Cash and she looked back at me before we both walked up the stairs. I went to Braylen's room and pulled him into my arms. I walked into me and Cash's bedroom and sat at the foot of the bed. She looked up at me and slightly smiled.

"May I hold him?" she asked like I would object.

I leaned back and handed her the baby. She began rubbing the top of his head and studying him.

The chain, I thought, lifting from the bed, and moved to my dresser.

I pulled the red velvet box from my drawer, and then walked back over to where she sat. I handed her the box, and she smiled, but looked puzzled. Using one hand to open it because she was cradling Braylen with the other one, she began to beam.

"Oh my God! Brook!" she cooed in her little voice.

TRAP GYRL 3

I stood back and smiled. She laid the baby down next to BJ. She jumped up and ran into my arms.

"I love it! Thank you."

"You're welcome, ma." I reached down and kissed her.

"Man, go take them to the room, ma. Daddy need some loving." I kissed her forehead.

"How about we leave them here and go take us a bath?"

"You ain't gotta tell me twice."

She lifted up and went to run the water. I patted Braylen back to sleep and kissed both my sons on the top of their heads, and then headed downstairs to the bar to get a bottle of 1738 Remy. I jogged back upstairs to my little mama and joined her in the bathroom. By the time I walked in, she was fully naked and inside the tub. The tub wasn't filled so she left it running. I peeled out my clothes and climbed on the opposite side from her. I poured us a cup and then handed her hers.

A nigga was finally happy. I had my baby back. Boy, I missed the shit out of her. Despite the bullshit we've been through, I missed her ass. Looking into her big beautiful eyes made me smile.

Barbie Scott
TRAP GYRL 3

She was gorgeous, which made me think about the fuck nigga she almost gave my loving too.

"Cash, you fucked that nigga?" I asked with my jaw clenched tight.

"No. I'll be honest, though, the night you kidnapped BJ, I was on my way to his crib. I don't know if I would have fucked him, but I just knew I was through with you. So, hey, there was a possibility."

"You attracted to him?"

"I mean, yeah. He's cute but he's not you, Nino."

"Nino, huh?" I smiled, but I was kind of hurt from her honesty. "Do you have plans on still seeing him?"

"Do you want me to? I mean, do you want your space or something so you can do you?"

"Hell nah, ma. I want my family back. I went to the limit of killing my son's mother. I did that shit because I knew with her out the picture, I would have you back."

"Do you regret it?"

"Hell nah. I mean, Braylen not having his mother is the only thing I think about, but fuck that, Cash, he got you. Are you gonna step up to the plate and help me with him?"

Barbie Scott
TRAP GYRL 3

She didn't respond verbally, she simply nodded her head, yes.

Looking at her nice perfect titties, sitting over the bubbles, made my dick rise. I began stroking my dick. Cash's freaky ass liked that shit so I knew I had her full attention. The lust in her eyes let me know I had her. I was also happy, because I didn't want the subject of Arcelie coming up nor did I want to bring up her and Que. Those were two things I wanted to bury in our past. I wanted to move forward and start planning another wedding.

Cash stood up from the water and pulled my hand so I could stand up. She then pushed me down so I could sit on the railing. The water running down her honey-colored complexion had a nigga dick hard as Chinese mathematics.

Damn, she's sexy, I thought as she stood in front of me and then dropped to her knees. She took my rock-hard dick into her mouth, coming back up with her tongue, swirling it around the tip. She got it nice and wet then went all the way down without any gagging. I ain't gone lie, she had me growling out like a straight hoe. I held onto the tub and had to slightly lift my body up. She had a nigga ready to jump through the roof.

Barbie Scott
TRAP GYRL 3

Finally, I was able to contain myself. I grabbed her head and began fucking her mouth. I laid my head back and closed my eyes. I was tryna think of football, money, hell, anything to keep from nutting. I kept my eyes shut and waited till my baby took me to ectacy.

***

Two weeks down, Cash and I were doing great. We were about to hit Juice tonight with the team, so right now, we were chilling with the babies. Ever since the day the Detectives showed up about Tiffany's murder, Cash had stepped up to the plate to help with Braylen. She did everything for him as if she birthed him. Having two babies around the house was crazy, but with each other's help, and Ms. Rosa, we were doing great.

Cash was in the kitchen whipping up some meatloaf, greens, mashed potatoes, and corn bread. She had it smelling so good, it only made me hungrier. My baby was the Jack of all Trades. She knew how to shoot a gun, she could kick a nigga ass, whip up dope with a blindfold on, and cooked meals like a chef. If I ever lost Cash, I'd be sick. It's

TRAP GYRL 3

like God created her for me and I'd die before I let her go or any other nigga have her.

I walked from upstairs and was caught mid-stride at the sight of her beauty. She was dressed in a pair of Nike gym shorts and the halter top to match. The high bun she wore graced her face as she moved around the dining area, setting up the dinner table. When she felt my presence, she turned around, holding the napkins, and then smiled. She began blushing with her shyness and that shit drove me crazy. The way her ass was sitting up in them shorts had a nigga ready to attack, but for now, I would let her be.

I walked into the den to check on the boys. Braylen was chilling in his bouncer, while BJ was in his high chair, staring dead at the TV. He was all into Blaze and the Monster Machines as if he was twelve instead of almost six months. BJ was so wrapped up into television, he didn't even acknowledge me. It was crazy how he was so into with the program. I jumped in front of the TV to get his attention. He looked around my left side then my right to keep from missing any parts. When he saw I wasn't moving, he began laughing and slamming his hands into the high chair.

Barbie Scott
TRAP GYRL 3

When I finally cut him some slack, I walked over to him and began rubbing my hands through his wild curly hair. My little man was the shit. Cash must couldn't stand me because he looked exactly like my baby pictures.

Cash walked into the den, drying her hands. She began smiling at how BJ was so in tuned with the TV. She walked over and grabbed Braylen out his bouncer and headed to the kitchen. When I picked BJ up, he playfully hit me in the head while laughing. Once we got into the kitchen, we took our seat and began eating. I kept BJ on my lap so I could feed him while Cash fed Bray his bottle. Just watching my little family warmed my heart and this was exactly how it would always be.

Chapter XVII

Que

Dear Quintin,

I know you're upset with me. Hopefully, one day, you'll forgive me. I'm currently in rehabilitation out of the city. I know it's not enough to make you forgive me, but it's a start. I'm getting my shit together for the sake of my daughter so I could get her out the system. I truly apologize about everything. I never meant for this shit to get so bad that I would put you or my child in this type of situation. I know I'm the one to blame, but you play a big part in this too. The entire time I loved you, you were in love with someone who didn't give two fucks about you. If she loved you, then why weren't you the one? Why did she marry Nino? And, not to mention, you ran off and had a baby by another woman. You pushed me into using drugs, Que. I needed something to numb the pain because liquor didn't help. I know you're probably busy right now

Barbie Scott
TRAP GYRL 3

so I'll let you be. The address is on the envelope if you still wanna kill me. Maybe I deserve to die!

Keisha...

Reading Keisha's letter did something to me. As much as I hated her and wanted her dead, I couldn't bring myself to do it. I was happy she was trying to get clean because Qui needed her mother. My baby girl loved Keisha to death. I always paid attention at how Qui's eyes would light up every time she was around her mother. I know I played a big part in her getting hooked on drugs, I just never wanted to admit it. I left the dope around her and I know I stressed her the fuck out. I read the short letter over and over, and each time, I was crushed, but happy. I contemplated going to the facility to kill her ass but I thought against it.

I met with the child custody attorney. We had a court date coming up for Qui. I paid the parenting class teacher a rack to sign my paperwork, so I knew for sure I would be getting my baby girl back in no time.

The conversation I had with Mario, over the phone, reigned heavy on my mind. After he told me Stephanie was dead, that shit low key hurt a nigga. I

TRAP GYRL 3

knew it could have only been Cash's ass that played a part in her death, but where the fuck was my seed? What really got me, was when Mario said he wasn't the one who had shot me and Bree, so that shit was eating me alive.

I walked upstairs to find Bree, she was knocked out at the foot of the bed. I slightly shook her because I needed to holler at her.

"Wake up, ma." I shook her again.

She finally opened her eyes and looked at me like I was crazy for disturbing her sleep.

"I need to holler at you, ma."

"What's wrong?" she asked, looking worried.

"The day we got shot, did you get a chance to see the shooter?"

The moment I asked, her eyes bulged almost out of her sockets.

"No," she said, sadly, but I could tell she was lying.

"Bree, I'm not gonna ask you again."

She looked away from me, and then began playing with her nails, but her eyes told it all.

"Bronx," she spoke just above a whisper, now confirming what I had figured.

I jumped to my feet and punched the wall so hard, it felt like my knuckles were broken.

Barbie Scott
TRAP GYRL 3

Bree began to cry but that shit didn't faze me one bit.

I stormed out the room, in a rage. I wasn't upset with her but the situation itself was just crazy. I ran into the kitchen to grab my car keys because I had to go holla at Cash, anyway. I would deal with this nigga Carter on my own, but right now, I needed answers about some whole other shit.

"Where are you going, Que?" Bree ran into the living room with a tear stained face.

"I'm about to go handle some business, Bree," I said, trying not to look at her.

"So, what now, Quintin?" she cried harder.

"Man, that's nothing you and I should be discussing, ma."

"The hell if it's not. That's my fucking brother!" she began crying like she was in one of those movies.

I just looked at her. My heart was hurting for her because she had already been through enough.

"Well, did your brother think about that when he almost took our lives, Breelah?"

She just stared at me and began shaking her head.

I walked out the door and headed to my ride.

Barbie Scott
TRAP GYRL 3

"But, you tried to kill him first, Que!" Bree shouted after me.

I was stopped in my tracks. I looked back and I was more than sure my eyes told it all. Bree and I locked eyes, but I was lost for words.

How the fuck does she know about that?

I ignored her. I then got into my ride and left, heading straight to Juice.

I pulled up to Juice, parked, and headed inside the club. I was moving so fast, I didn't even bother stopping for everyone that was calling my name. When I made up to the VIP, I walked into Cash's section where the whole crew was turning up. I dapped Blaze and the rest of the crew and went straight to Cash.

"Cash, can I holla at you?" I asked her.

She looked up at me from glossy eyes like she was buzzed. She seemed kind of hesitant but she got up and told me to follow her into her office. When we walked off, Nino was looking at me kind of funny. The look alone told me that he knew about what went down with me and Cash, but shit, he had some explaining to do too.

When we walked in Cash's office, she took a seat on top of her desk and I sat on the sofa directly in front of her.

Barbie Scott
TRAP GYRL 3

"Where my baby at, ma?" I got straight to the point.

"What?" she asked like she didn't know what the fuck I was talking about.

"The baby by Stephanie, Cash. I already know it was you that killed her, I just wanna know where's my kid?"

"I'm sorry, Que, but you kn…"

I cut her off.

"Damn, was it a girl or boy?"

"A girl," she said.

I nodded my head.

"We left her at the hospital," she said, making my jaw clench.

The moment she said that, I sighed in relief. I nodded my head and got up to leave. I really wanted to stay and fuck with the crew, but I had somewhere very important to be.

I walked out without another word and headed to my whip, in deep thought. I couldn't even be mad at Cash for killing Stephanie. That bitch had come into our lives with ulterior motives and Cash played a big part in it all.

Now that I knew my baby was safe, I hopped on the highway, heading for the hotel.

Barbie Scott
TRAP GYRL 3

When I walked into the room, she was sitting on the bed, fully naked. I was going to hit this bad ass bitch and put everything in my life behind me. Bree was blowing up my phone, but right now, she too would get put on the back burner. This shit I was doing right now wasn't personal, it was strictly business; yes, I had business with my dick as well.

"You missed this dick?"

"Yes, papi. I've missed you so much," she spoke in her very heavy accent.

"Well, bend over and let me show you how much I missed this pussy."

Chapter XVIII

Cash Lopez

When I walked back into the club area, Brook was giving me a cold mean mug. At first, I thought it was because of Que, but hell no, not even. Nina was sitting in the VIP across from us with Dez. Jah had walked in their section as I began to shit bullets. I prayed this nigga wouldn't say shit to me because Brook would indeed die. I couldn't help but smirk because Nina was bold as fuck. Because Carlos was heavy in the crew now, I knew he would walk in at any moment; I just prayed they wouldn't tear my club up.

I walked up on Brook and gave him an insuring kiss. His face softened a little but I knew that was bullshit. I walked over and poured me another glass of Dusse. I needed to get buzzed because I knew shit could get out of hand tonight, and I wanted to be numb. I then walked over to my girls and began the gossip of the night. Diane and I kept laughing and making silly faces at Nina while she was in the other section. She walked into our section and the entire time we talked, Brook was all in our grill.

"Bitch, who is them fine ass niggas?" Diane asked, doing her little ratchet dance.

"That's Cash's..." Nina went to say but I cut her off.

"They are cute, that's Nina's boo right there, and that's his homie, who is very single." I pointed at Jah.

"Well bitch, hook me up!" Diane laughed.

Nina looked at me, but I simply raised my glass to let her know it was a go. Even though I liked Jah, and he was the kind of man I could see myself with, I was already taken and there was no reason to let a good piece of nigga go to waste. I mean, we never had sex, and Diane deserved a good nigga like Jah.

Nina and Diane headed over to Jah's VIP. Diane wasted no time macking in on Jah. He looked at me, puzzled, so I shrugged my shoulders to let him know I wasn't tripping. He looked so disappointed, but it is what it is.

I walked over and took a seat next to Blaze and Tiny, and began making small talk with them. Every now and then, I would steal a peek over at Nina and Diane. I prayed Jah would be comfortable and understanding with our new arrangements. Had

TRAP GYRL 3

it been any other chick, I wouldn't have played things the way I did, but I felt Diane was fit for him.

For the rest of the night, I fooled with Brook. The club was going smooth so I knew I could relax and enjoy myself. When Nina, Diane, Jah, and Dez got up to leave, that relaxed me more. I grabbed the bottle and kicked back, knowing Carlos wouldn't come in trying to kill my best friend.

***

The next few weeks breezed by smoothly. Brook and I were back to normal, raising our boys. Brook had never mentioned anything about Que and I, so I was sure Bree hadn't told on me. I prayed she wouldn't because I knew Brook would go crazy and right now, things had seemed to go back to normal.

Today, Brook was staying home with the boys so I could go have lunch with my girls. First, we were going to take some flowers to Niya's gravesite, and then we were going to head to a restaurant on the beach for mimosa's.

Lately, Nina and Diane had been chilling with Jah and Dez, and today, they were going to fill me in. Diane seemed to really like Jah, and I was happy for her. Jah had text me a couple of times talking

TRAP GYRL 3

shit about me pawning him off on my friend but after explaining to him how I felt, he eased up.

    After sliding into my one piece red romper I had gotten from Nina's boutique, I put on my three inch strappy Gucci sandals. I eyed myself in my mirror, and thanks to BJ, he had giving me a bigger ass. The waist trainer I wore constantly was helping me get my normal waist size back. I wore my hair in a high bun and made sure to hook up my baby hair. Satisfied with my look, I headed out the door and to my ride. Brook was giving Braylen a bath so I hurried to leave before he began calling my name like he was crazy.

    ***

    Finally making it to the restaurant, I was now at ease. The gravesite was hard for me and my girls. We cried, laughed, cried, laughed, and cried some more. This shit was hard for us to deal with and we vowed to always visit our friend. Nathine was still upset with me but her money hungry ass accepted every dollar I wired into her account. She didn't even bother to call and say thank you, but I didn't sweat it because that was the least I could do.

Barbie Scott
TRAP GYRL 3

"What appetizers do you want, Cash?" Tiny asked, knocking me out my thoughts.

"Umm, I'll take oysters and a shrimp cocktail."

I looked up at the waitress whose name was Carmen. I loved coming to this restaurant because we were always treated like royalty, and of course, we didn't have to pay for a thing. They had great food and very decent hospitality; Not to just us but to everyone that visited.

"Cash, so when were you gonna tell me you and Jah talked?" Diane asked, catching me by surprise.

"It wasn't shit, ma. You know I'd tell you."

"But, its awkward. I mean, I'm not tripping because he told me nothing ever happened, but damn, ma," she said, slightly shaking her head.

"Do you kinda like him, still?"

"Nah, not at all. However, I do have one request," I smirked. "I just wanna watch yall fuck."

The moment I said that, they all laughed. I was dead ass serious, though. Because I couldn't have a piece, I wanted to at least see what I would be missing. I was a cold freak and that type of shit turned me on. There was no funny shit with me and Diane, but I knew her freaky ass would let me watch.

TRAP GYRL 3

"Yo ass is serious too, huh?" Nina said, already knowing how I am.

"Okay, you got that," Diane said, laughing, but I could tell she was dead ass about me watching.

When our food came, we began diving in. I noticed Tiny picking through her food, which reminded me.

"So, yo ass still ain't got rid of that baby?" I asked her and she looked embarrassed.

"It's difficult." She shook her head. "A part of me wants to keep it, then a part of me wants to get rid of it. I just don't know if I'm ready for another baby. Then, a part of me wanna give Blaze his first child, so I don't know," she spoke, and her eyes began to water.

We all looked at her in awe.

I understood her point from both angles. The life we were living was a crazy one, but hell, that's probably what Blaze needed to slow his ass down. Tiny was supposed to be his rock, but instead, her ass was his Bonnie.

"I think you should have it, ma. Blaze needs something to slow his ass down. Plus, he need something to leave on this earth before he's gone."

"Yeah, you're right. I'ma give it some more thought, then I'll tell him." She finally smiled.

TRAP GYRL 3

"So, what's up with you and Dez?" I focused my attention on Nina.

"That's my boo right there," she squealed. "Dick A-1 too," she laughed.

I guess she really ain't fucking with Carlos, I thought as I smiled.

The waiter walked up and sat another two bottles of Ace on our table and a whole pitcher of orange juice. We wasted no time pouring our drinks and continued our girl talk.

I looked down at my ringing phone and had a text from an unknown number. When I opened the message, it read.

Just checking in with you. I'm doing straight, my Gutta Babi.

That's good to know. When are you gonna finally come see us, nigga, we miss you.

I'll be there soon, ma. And, I miss y'all too. WYD (what you doing) right now?

Right here with the girls, having lunch.

Fasho, tell them I said what's up. "

"Carter said what's up, girls," I told the girls and at the same time, they all smiled and cooed "Hiii, Carter," making us all laugh.

But, I'ma let you go. I'll holla soon, ma.

Okay, and be safe.

Always. (smiley face emoji)
"What's up with that nigga, Cash?" Nina asked.
"Girl, ain't no tellin with Carter's ass. I know he need to come see his damn sister." I shook my head and picked up my glass. It was something up with this nigga, but for now, I would let it go.
What's in the dark always came to the light.

Chapter XIX

Diane

Cash's ass was crazy as hell. I couldn't help but laugh at her drunk ass as she followed me into my condo. Her crazy ass was dead serious about watching Jah and I have sex. I knew she wouldn't join because she was back with Nino and she wasn't with the threesome shit, anyway. I placed the call to Jah and told him I was ready. I didn't mention Cash to him because I didn't want him to feel awkward. I was really digging Jah, and I hoped he felt the same

TRAP GYRL 3

way. We talked, we text, and even went out a few times. Today would be our first time having sex. I just prayed Cash would get her rocks off and leave because I needed a one on one with him.

Cash's ass was drunk so I knew how she could be when she would drink. She ignored her phone for the umpteenth time, and I was sure it was Brook. She finally answered and told him she was at my house.

While she was on the phone with him, I ran into the restroom to take a shower and get sexy. By the time I was done, Jah had sent me a text, telling me he was out front. I didn't know why, but I had gotten kind of nervous. Cash was on the balcony, smoking a blunt, and drinking another mimosa she got from my fridge.

When I got to the door, Jah was already there looking fine as hell. The smell of his cologne tingled my nose and made me crave his ass more. I don't know if it was the liquor talking or was he looking that good because I was now ready to get this show on the road. I led him upstairs to my bedroom and told him to get comfortable.

"You're looking sexy, ma." He smiled a sexy smile.

Barbie Scott
TRAP GYRL 3

I blushed and then went to pour him a cup of
Hennessy.

When I came back into the room, he had kicked
his shoes off and his Robin jeans were now folded
neatly on my nightstand. He had on a wife beater
and I couldn't help but admire his body. It was
perfect. I lit a few candles around the room to set
the mood then sat next to him on the bed. I took a
swig of my drink and then kicked my legs up over
his. When he began to massage my feet, I let out a
slight moan. This is exactly what I needed to come
home to every night; tonight, I hoped things would
go further.

Not being able to contain myself any more, I
slid his briefs off. He watched closely as he took a
drink from his cup. Once I had his shirt off, I placed
soft kisses from his neck down to his love stick. By
the time I made it down there, his dick was rock
hard. My eyes shot wide open at the sight of him.
This man had to have the biggest dick I'd ever seen
in my life. Whoever said tall,I shot slim niggas had
more dick, lied. Because this man was big, buff, and
packing a monster.

I picked up my remote and pressed play on my
playlist to drown out the now slurping sounds from
me giving him some intense head. Chris Brown -

Barbie Scott
TRAP GYRL 3

Medusa (Seduce Her) began to play thru my speakers.

The sound of my ass being slapped made Jah and I look up. I almost forgot Cash was even here, I was so caught up in the moment. She gave Jah a seductive smile then sat in the chair directly across from the bed with the entire bottle of champagne in her hand. Jah looked puzzled but I guess he wasn't tripping because I had kept going.

I took his entire dick into my mouth and sucked like my life depended on it. He was shaved perfectly and I could still smell the body wash he had used. He smelled so good and it made me devour him. When I looked at him, he looked from Me to Cash, and then back to me. I had him sissing as if any moment he would cum.

He pulled back and told me to stand up. I did as told, and he bent me over the bed and entered me from behind. I tried to run but he pulled me back. He began stroking me with strong and powerful strokes, making me moan loudly. I looked over at Cash, who now had her hands in her pants, fingering herself. I could tell this shit was turning her on. She watched on, with so much fire in her eyes. I don't know why, but this shit was making me hornier. My pussy was dripping wet.

"This what you want to see, Cash?" he asked her as he plunged in and out of me, roughly.

She didn't speak a word, except for the moans she let out that sounded like cries. She picked up her ringing phone and began reading the text that had come through. As for me, I kept getting the life fucked out of me.

Nina...

Dez was out cold from this lethal pussy I had put on him. I couldn't wait for him to fall asleep because I wanted to go through his phone to see who he's been texting the entire time we were together. When I scrolled through his most recent text, my eyes shot open at what I was reading.

Me: *I'm with her now. Jah and I had met them at the restaurant but Cash left because I guess that nigga Nino kept texting her.*
Uncle M: *Good. Time is almost running out. Y'all keep doing y'all but be careful because Cash is a smart bitch.*

Reading the text, I began crying, silently. I tried my hardest to not wake him up, and at this point, I

TRAP GYRL 3

didn't know what to do. I shot Cash a text because I knew she was with Jah and Diane.

Me: Aye, ma. Punch this number in your phone and tell me who's number it is (305) 555-4635
Best Friend: *That Mario's, why?*
Me: Bitch, we been set up. These niggas is Mario's nephews. Get out of there.
Best Friend: *Get out of there, Nina.*

I sent Blaze a text and told him to get to my house, fast. I didn't have anyone else to call. I was now scared and my body began to shake. I quietly lifted out the bed, making sure I didn't wake Dez and went into the bathroom. I sat on the toilet and cried my eyes out. I was now so scared, I prayed Blaze would hurry up. I didn't want to alarm Dez so I got myself together and went back into the room.

When I opened the door, I was staring down the barrel of a nine millimeter. I shook my head and cursed myself for being so damn naive. He had his phone in his hand and was looking at the messages I had read.

"This what happens when you snoop, ma. You know what they say, you seek, you shall find," he said with pure hatred in his eyes.

Barbie Scott
TRAP GYRL 3

"Why, Dez?" I cried out. I knew my life was over but I needed answers.

"It's how the game goes, ma. I ain't gone front, you got some good pussy, but business is business, baby."

"So, you are Mario's nephew?"

"Yep, my dad's brother. What yall thought, we liked y'all for real? I mean, don't get me wrong if this was another lifetime, I would have wifed yo pretty ass." He picked my clothes up from the floor and told me to get dressed.

"Where are we going?"

"Shit, ain't no need to keep pretending since you know, now. You about to take me to Cash and I'ma kill you bitches together."

"And, how do you think you're gonna get passed her security?"

"That's for you to figure out. And, any funny shit, you're dead," he said with much aggression.

Once I was done dressing, he walked me outside with his gun pointed at my head. I had to think and think quick. My phone was in the bathroom so I couldn't call anybody. It had been about thirty minutes since I text Blaze so I prayed he would pull up by the time we got to the car. When I opened the door, and rounded the corner, I

Barbie Scott
TRAP GYRL 3

quickly ducked because Blaze had his gun aimed and ready.

Pop!

Dez dropped from the single shot that was let off.

Thank God for silencers, I thought because we were outside my home.

Blaze dragged Dez back inside, and right on my living room floor, he put three more bullets into Dez's head to finish him off. He quickly hopped on his phone and called the body bag boys to come clean up the mess. I shot Cash a text to see was she straight and after a few minutes, we finally got a reply, saying she was straight and heading to the warehouse. Blaze and I jumped into his whip and sped to the warehouse to meet her.

Chapter XX

Cash Lopez

Watching Jah fuck the shit out of Diane had me ready to go home and make love to Brook. I can't even front, Jah was working with a Mandingo dick that had me in awe. The way he was stroking her made my pussy drip more and more. There he was, eyeing me while he was stroking her, and that made my insides jitter. I began fingering myself as I envisioned it was me getting my back blew out.

The sound of my text alert broke my trance. I was going to ignore it, assuming it was Brook, but to my surprise, it was Nina. Reading her text made me lose my whole train of thought. I reached into my purse with ease then stood up and walked towards Jah and Diane. The gleam in his eyes must have told him I was going to join in, but I had a surprise for this nigga. I seductively walked over to the bed, and no lie, I had to get one good feel of this dick before I would do the unthinkable. I reached

over and grabbed his dick, making him stop his
strokes. He looked me in my eyes with so much
passion but it was all an act. I kissed him
aggressively and when I pulled back, his eyes were
still closed as if he was savoring the moment. I put
the cold steel to his head and it made him open his
eyes.

"Boom!" I shot him in between the eyes.

Diane jumped up and began crying. She didn't
know what the fuck was going on. I fired a few
more shots into his body and when I knew he was
dead, I looked at Diane.

"Mario's nephew," I said just above a whisper
and she gasped.

She covered her mouth with her hand, in
disbelief.

"Look on the bright side, you got some good
dick out of it, ma," I said, and went to retrieve my
phone. I placed a call to the body bag boys to get
the mess cleaned up. Nina had sent me a text to let
me know she was with Blaze so I told them to meet
me at the warehouse.

On the way to the warehouse, Diane and I cried
together. I wasn't crying out of fear, I cried because
shit was serious. That was a close call and we
couldn't afford any more slip ups. These niggas had

gotten in good, and boy, was that a close call.
What's crazy is I could tell that Jah was really
catching feelings for me and I was sure he was
having second thoughts about it all; or was he? The
streets had been too damn quiet but I knew that after
today it was about to go up. My crew and I had
bodied not only Mario's daughter but two of his
nephews and right-hand man as well. I don't know
what Mario was thinking, but this nigga was
jeopardizing his entire family and didn't seem to
give two fucks. I couldn't wait to get my hands on
this nigga. I wasn't done with him. Once I had his
head, I would be satisfied and could move on with
my life. Mario's crew was weak as fuck. Without
the head, the snake couldn't survive, and that's
exactly what he was the head of his organization. If
he died, then the crew would die along with him.
His entire crew knew how powerful my family was,
but Mario didn't seem to care one bit.

When we pulled up to the warehouse, Blaze
and Nina were already here. Diane and I stepped out
the car and went inside. The two of them were
sitting in their normal spots as if we were
conducting a crew meeting. I looked at Nina, and I
could tell she had been crying. I can't say I didn't

Barbie Scott
TRAP GYRL 3

feel her pain because, in fact, I did. These niggas had gotten close, a little too close.

"Man, y'all bitches 'bout to get killed thinking with y'all pussy," Blaze said, shaking his head.

I knew he didn't mean anything by calling us out of our names, and honestly, we deserved it. We let these sexy ass niggas come into our worlds, forgetting we had enemies. It was crazy because they seemed harmless but that shit was a disguise. Them niggas was Mario's fucking family.

***

Once we discussed our business, Blaze headed home and Nina, Diane, and I went to me and Brook's house. It was 4:30 in the morning and I knew I wouldn't hear the end of it. I knew I would have to tell Brook what happened but I'd be sure to leave out the part about me killing Jah while I played with my pussy, watching him and my friend fuck.

When we walked into the house, just as I expected, Brook was wide awake playing his NBA2k with both babies on the side of him in their bouncers. I knew he would be mad, but once I told him what happened, I was sure he would lighten up.

Barbie Scott
TRAP GYRL 3

He didn't even bother to look up. He ignored us but
I guess the sound of Nina's weeps made him finally
look up. Because he was acting like a dick, I told
the girls let's go lay down. I went into my room and
found some PJ's for Nina and Diane. Once I gave
them the garments, everyone headed for separate
restrooms to shower.

After my shower, I went back downstairs to get
BJ and laid him down in his room. Brook was still
ignoring the shit out of me, so I went into the room
with the girls who were still awake, smoking a
blunt. I joined in because I knew the weed would
help me sleep.

We began discussing the guys we had to get rid
of, but making sure we kept it down so Brook
wouldn't hear. I had gotten a text from the Body
Bag Boys, letting me know both houses were
straight. After not being able to take it anymore, I
went up to the room and passed out the moment my
head hit the pillow.

When I finally opened my eyes, it was almost
two in the afternoon. I couldn't believe I had slept
this long. I lifted out my bed and went into the
restroom to handle my hygiene. I then went
downstairs and found Nina and Diane at the
counter, eating.

Barbie Scott
TRAP GYRL 3

"We were wondering when were you gonna wake up," Nina said, smiling. Diane handed me my plate out the microwave and I was glad because I was starving.

"Ohhh, who cooked this?" I asked because Brook's chef was nowhere in sight.

"Nino," Diane laughed.

"Y'all bitches ain't let him poison me, did yall?" I asked, and we all laughed. They knew I was joking so they didn't bother answering.

"When I'm ready to kill yo ass, I'll just split yo wig with my strap," Brook said, coming into the kitchen. I figured he was gone already because he was nowhere in sight, but I guess I was wrong.

"Boy, you know I ain't worried 'bout you," I smirked.

He joined us at the counter and took a seat directly across from me. I don't know why, but for some reason, he was grilling us.

"So, y'all ready to tell me what happened last night?" he asked.

Damn, who these niggas work for, me or him? I thought to myself because I knew either Blaze told or the Body Bag Boys had told him what happened.

"Well, as you know, Cash hooked Diane up with Jah. After we went to the cemetery, then out to eat, we all went our separate ways. Cash was headed home; Diane and Jah had gone to her crib and Dez and I went to my house. After I fuc... I mean, after we chilled, he fell asleep. Something told me to go through his phone, so I did. I saw texts between him and Mario so I shot Cash a text and told her. I then hit Blaze, and of course, he came to my rescue. Cash went to Diane's and she was also her savior." Nina shook her head as Brook listened.

Diane and I looked at each other and we tried our hardest to keep from laughing. To my surprise, Brook didn't hit us with some sarcastic bullshit. He only listened and shook his head.

"Well, I'm glad y'all straight. I can't tell y'all what to do with yall pussies, but next time, let the crew know so we could do a full background check on niggas."

Everyone shook their heads, but me.

"I know y'all don't wanna do it, but I think it's safe if y'all take a couple guards with y'all, at all times. We've bodied to many of Mario's family members so I know when he strikes, he's gonna try and hit hard. Also, I think it's safe if y'all go stay at Ms. Lopez's crib for a couple of weeks. I already hollered at her so y'all good."

Barbie Scott
TRAP GYRL 3

Again, we all shook our heads in understanding.

"Y'all could stay here for a few days, though, and keep Cash company, because her ass on restriction for a while. Y'all need to get some clothes, I got four guards that are gonna take y'all. This won't be for long, y'all, just let us figure some shit out with this nigga, Mario. It ain't no telling what them fuck niggas told they uncle," and with that, he stood to his feet. He looked me square in my face and then turned to walk away. Before he was out of earshot, I called out to him.

"Brooklyn, I love you," I spoke in all honesty.

"I love you more, Cash Lopez," he smirked and headed out the door.

Once we were done eating, I went to get the babies from upstairs then brought them downstairs to chill with us. It had begun to rain hard this morning and it looked like it wasn't going to let up anytime soon, so the girls decided to get their clothing later. We all went into the den along with the babies and lit the fireplace. We agreed on Mean Girls to watch on the projector and poured us all a glass of wine. After everything we were into last night, we decided to just chill and be thankful we were still alive.

Barbie Scott
TRAP GYRL 3

Chapter XXI

Brooklyn Nino

3 Months Later...

The streets have been quiet since the bullshit with Cash and her friends. They had stayed with us a few days as planned, then moved into Ms. Lopez's mansion. She didn't mind it because she was always staying at Esco's house, so her house was pretty lonely. Cash had moved her stuff back in my crib but she would go over Ms. Lopez's house just about every day to chill with her friends. Ms. Lopez's crib was the safest house because her security was heavy. Even though the Cartel wasn't making much noise, them niggas were never ones to underestimate. I knew, eventually, they would try some shit and we couldn't take any more losses.

For the last few months, I had been in the traps more. Kellz was still holding shit down but he had a

TRAP GYRL 3

baby on the way so the few niggas I put inside to replace him needed to be supervised. Now that Kellz was away more, I had to cook my work and drop it off myself. I had a strong little team outside of Cash and her team, but one thing I didn't do was trust too many people. I needed to see my bread and even count it myself. Especially since BJ's birthday was two months away, and his party alone cost almost sixty grand. My little man was finally about to be one-year-old, and I couldn't wait until he started walking. He was holding on to the tables but that nigga wouldn't take a step for shit. Braylen was now sitting up and holding his bottle, perfectly. He looked so much like Tiffany, that shit had me feeling bad every time I looked at him.

"I'm ready for you, Nino," Naomi said, knocking me out my thoughts.

I walked over to her styling chair and handed her BJ. She strapped him to the chair, and to my surprise, he didn't even cry. Once he was secure, I headed outside to make a few business calls about the restaurant. I was ready to expand my shit and get another location in Cali. I also had signed paperwork, putting the restaurant in BJ's name. I had Braylen a nice little stash put up so his little ass would be straight. I chose to give the restaurant to

Barbie Scott
TRAP GYRL 3

BJ because he was my first born. It was named after my mother and it held a sentimental value to me and my family, outside of the money it made.

After I was done on my calls, I stuck my head in the door to look at BJ. The sucker Naomi had given him had his little ass quiet and content. When I turned around, I was shocked to see the thots of the century; Monique and Arcelie. They both eye fucked me something vicious, but I ignored them hoes.

"Oh, you can't speak, Nino?" Monique asked, stepping into my personal space.

"Back yo ass up, Hoenique," I called her by her around the way name.

She brushed it off and went to say something else.

"Yeah, let me show you what a real hoe could do. Let me and my girl give you one night of pleasure with us," she smirked over at Arcelie. Arcelie didn't say much but the look on her face told it all. She wanted this dick just as bad as Mo, but nope, these hoes weren't getting this dick; not anymore, at least.

"Nah, I'm smooth," I said and walked back into the shop.

Barbie Scott
TRAP GYRL 3

When Mo followed behind and took a seat at the booth across from Naomi, I couldn't help but laugh because she was now working in this shop.

Almost two hours later, BJ was finally done. I paid Naomi and headed out the door. I needed to get far away from Monique and Celie because them hoes was eye fucking me the entire time I was in there. After what Cash had done to them hoes, I was surprised them hoes even had the audacity to speak.

I buckled BJ in his car seat and quickly hopped in. I turned on Paw Patrol on the flip down for him because it was his favorite show. We hopped on the highway and headed to Ms. Lopez's crib to surprise Cash with his new hairdo.

When we pulled up, I noticed Blaze and Que's car.

What they got going on? I thought, getting out the car.

When we walked in the front door, the living room was empty, however, you could hear loud voices and noise coming from the den. I headed towards the noise, and of course, Cash was the loudest one. When I walked in, these muthafuckas had a big ass dice game going on. They were in a big ass huddle and it had to be about twenty g's on the ground. There were empty Hennessy bottles on

TRAP GYRL 3

the bar and it looked like a Cheech and Chong movie from all the smoke. Cash was so focused on the game, she never saw us come in.

"Let me get a five or nine, she hit?" Nina asked the crowd.

"Bet!" Que said, dropping some money.

"Oh my God, Nino!" Tiny yelled and ran over, taking BJ out my hand.

Everyone stopped and looked at us then burst out into laughter. Cash stood up and hit me with a smirk. She was smiling and shaking her head at the same time. I mean, what she thought? Shit, BJ was a Carter boy.

"For real, baby. Dreads?" Cash laughed.

"Yeah, ma. It was time, he about to be one," I told her.

"He really looks just like yo ass now," Nina laughed and took him from Tiny.

After everyone talked about his hair for a while, I went to find Rosa so she could take him out the room. It was too much damn smoke and I'd be damned if my youngin caught a dirty; shit, you never know what could happen.

When I came back into the den, Breelah was nowhere, sitting next to Que. I walked over and gave her a hug, and then playfully punched her in

TRAP GYRL 3

her wounded arm. Everyone was still shooting dice,
and I wanted in. I pulled ten g's out my pocket
because that's all they were getting from me. Now,
don't get it fucked up, I had licks, but you never
knew with gambling.

***

Cash and I ended up staying at Ms. Lopez's
crib. I ran home and grabbed some more clothes for
Braylen and a pile of mail that was in the box. Once
I got back, I went into the den to chill with Cash
and Diane, who were watching television.

"Where's Nina ass at?" I asked the girls
because I didn't see her when I first walked in.

"She's with Carlos," Cash smirked.

"What, they back together?"

"No, he called her about Cashmere, talking
bout she misses her."

We all laughed.

I had to give it to Carlos. Since their break up,
he had been having his daughter and wouldn't let
her leave with Nina unless she was staying with
them. Every day, Carlos called me to check up on
Nina but he was doing him. I never told him about
what had happened with Nina and that Dez nigga

Barbie Scott
TRAP GYRL 3

because, even though Carlos and I had gotten pretty cool, our loyalty was with Nina.

I took a seat on the couch, next to Cash, and opened the big yellow envelope I had received. It was like déjà vu from the last time I opened an envelope and it contained a DVD of Cash and my brother, making out. I quickly shook the thoughts out my head and began reading.

By the time I was done, I was furious. It was custody paperwork from Ms. Scott, trying to get full custody of Braylen. It had a scheduled court date and this shit was fucked up. I understand her wanting to see her grandbaby, but damn, court? She could have gone about it a whole other way. I hated courts, and especially custody courts. I knew what happened in those muthafuckas. Ms. Scott would bring up my criminal history, and any other dirt she could find on me to get my son.

"What's wrong, Brook?" Cash asked, sounding concerned. I handed her the papers and looked off at the TV. After she was done reading them, she gasped loudly and covered her mouth with her hand, and shot me a crazy look.

"So, what we gone do? They can't just take him, Brooklyn. She is only the grandmother," she said as if she wanted to cry. Cash had pretty much

TRAP GYRL 3

been raising Braylen so I knew this shit would affect her just as much as it affected me.

"Honestly, ma, I'ma have my lawyer hit her up and see if we could work something out. Maybe shoot her some bread and visitation rights. We got too much shit on our plate right now to worry about this. And, I can't take the chances with my son. They gone get to digging up old shit on a nigga, and I can't have that."

"Yeah, you right," Cash said like she was on a verge of breaking down.

I kissed her on the forehead and told her don't stress. I would handle this old bitch in my own way and not through the punk ass white people.

Chapter XXII

Nina and Carlos

Whap! Carlos came into the room and slapped the shit out of me. I fell to the floor and grabbed my jaw. He stood over me and began shouting and calling me every name in the book. Ever since the day he picked me up from Ms. Lopez's house, I came home with him because he swore my baby missed me. Now, here we were, in an intense argument because he swore I gave him an STD. When I told him I haven't fucked him in two months, he swore on his mother, his dick was burning.

"So, you mean to tell me you walked around with a burning dick for two months, Los? Yeah, fucking right, nigga. And, if you put yo' fucking hands on me again, I'ma put a bullet in yo' stomach and you'll be wearing a shit bag for the rest of yo' life!"

TRAP GYRL 3

"Nina, I don't give a fuck what you say. Your hoe ass has been out there fucking some nigga named Dez. Is this my baby?" he had the nerves to ask me.

"You know what, let me get my shit so I could go. Give me my baby and take your nasty ass to the doctor, hoe! I'm done with this conversation."

"You ain't done with shit. Your nasty ass burnt me so you going with me to the doctor."

I couldn't do shit but shake my head at him. It was like every day I looked at him, he disgusted me. I was so done with this nigga, it wasn't even funny. What he failed to realize was, I'm a boss bitch, I got plenty money and I'm sexy as fuck. I'm not hard up for no nigga. I could bag any man that walked this earth. To keep it one real, he was pushing a little weight but I bossed his ass up.

Fuck a nigga mean? I thought to myself, watching him act a donkey's ass.

I went into the living room and grabbed my purse. This nigga wanted to be petty, I was going to be petty with his stupid ass.

"Come on, nigga, let's go," I said and walked out the door without giving him a chance to say another word.

Barbie Scott
TRAP GYRL 3

When we pulled up to the clinic, I walked in way ahead of him because he was still talking shit. I signed our names on the clipboard and took a seat to wait for the doctor. I made sure to sit far the fuck away from this nigga and even hopped on my phone to busy myself. Carlos kept shooting me mean mugs but I ignored him the entire time. I couldn't wait to get this shit done and over with. If I did have an STD, I had to more than likely get it from Dez, but then that would be dumb because I hadn't slept with Carlos since I had been messing with Dez. I wasn't a nasty ass bitch so had it been true, then I would have been come to take care of my pussy.

After about thirty-five minutes, our names were called and we were escorted to the back. Carlos was sent on one side of the room, and I was on the other. I made sure to close my curtain because I didn't even want to look at this nigga.

Once we were examined, we waited for the doctor to come in with our results. I ignored Carlos as much as I could. He was still talking shit and calling me all kinds of nasty bitches. I swear I was ready to put my gun in his mouth and tell him to shut the fuck up.

He better be lucky we're in this damn doctor's office, I thought right when the doctor walked in.

Barbie Scott
TRAP GYRL 3

"You two are still fussing?" The doc snickered. He had heard us going back and forth. Hell, I'm sure the entire office heard us and that was one of the reasons I tried my best to ignore him.

"What's up, doc, I gotta get up out of here," Carlos said like he had so much to do.

"Well, Mr. Hanson, you can't leave just yet. However, Miss., you're free to go."

"What the fuck you mean *she can go?*"

"Well, she tested negative on all STD's and you, sir, tested positive on Gonorrhea. You have to stay behind so we can give you a shot and explain the necessary steps."

Carlos didn't say a word. However, he wore a dumb ass look on his face.

"Nasty ass, nigga!" I shouted, jumping up from the bed. I began putting my clothes on and trying my best to hurry the fuck up.

"Nina, please, ma," he begged.

I ignored his ass because there wasn't much to say. I was done with this nigga and I was taking my daughter. Out of all the things to do to a woman, this had to be the worst shit. I know Carlos wasn't a nasty ass, careless nigga, and that only made me angrier. Whoever this bitch was, had him because he didn't protect himself with her. When I got with

TRAP GYRL 3

Carlos, we used condoms for months and we fucked every day. I didn't know rather to cry or laugh because this nigga had humiliated me for the last fucking time.

Once I was done dressing, I called Nino to send the security team to pick me up. On my way walking out, I bumped into the bitch, Monique. She was wearing a dumb ass smirk on her face. I just shook my head because that hoe stayed in the clinic. If it wasn't an abortion, it was an STD. Just the thought of it, I wouldn't be surprised if she was the one who burnt Carlos. I mean, she was cute and he was a man.

Shit, you never know.

Walking right past the bitch, she knew not to say shit to me. I let that little smirk slide because she was dealing with enough already, and I was sure that's why she was here.

Once the van pulled up to pick me up, I couldn't help but laugh because Nino had text me three times to ask have they came. It made me feel great inside that I had someone that cared about me that much. I mean, this nigga had sent three guards to pick me up.

I got comfortable in the far back and began browsing my phone. I kept taking sneak peeks at the

one on the passenger side because he was fine. I
didn't want to come off like a hoe, but got damn,
that nigga was fine. He looked to be about 6'2. He
had a nice size body and locks that hung shoulder
length. His earrings screamed baller and his
demeanor screamed gangsta.

Damn!

I scrolled through my Facebook page and
stopped on a status that caught my attention. It was
Monique's Facebook and she had written a status
about me.

What's on your mind?

*Seen ya girl, Nina, at the clinic. Yeah, that ass
on fire. (fire emoji)*

I wanted to tell these niggas to turn the van
around so bad, but I sucked it up. Underneath the
status was a comment. I clicked on it and it read.

Cash Lopez:
But you there too? Haha (fire emoji)

That's exactly why I loved my best friend. She
would get petty with a bitch in a minute. Since this
hoe wanted to play, I had something for her ass. I

TRAP GYRL 3

uploaded a pic of my results in the comments, with a comment that said, *Check the scoreboards, bitch.* (Laughing emoji).

Not even two minutes later, there were nine comments of people laughing, even Que's petty ass. I liked the comments and my phone started ringing. When I looked at the caller ID, it was Cash. I quickly answered and the gossip began. We laughed about Monique, and then I filled her in on the episode with Carlos. She told me exactly what I knew she would; leave his ass. She also told me if I went back to him, she wouldn't mad because that's how love went. I was shocked as hell by her statement. Not Cash Lopez, the one that dodges heartbreaks and bullets. My bestie had made a drastic change in her life and I was truly happy for her. We had been through so much, she deserved to be happy.

I couldn't wait to be happy, my damn self. I was done with Carlos, and after this shit with Dez, I was through with love for a while. I wasn't in love with Dez but I really liked him and saw myself with the fuck nigga. It was crazy because every time we were around each other, shit seemed so sincere. He seemed like he really liked me and I thought we had something.

Barbie Scott
TRAP GYRL 3

"Get yo' ass out, Nina," the sexy passenger said, bringing me from my trance.

He wore a slight smirk and jumped out to open my door. I smiled shyly as I hopped out and made my way towards the house.

"Leave these fuck niggas alone and get you a real nigga that's gone appreciate yo ass, ma," he said and jumped back into the van.

I stood there stunned as fuck. For the first time, I was left speechless. I watched the van pull off and was stuck watching them drive off until it was out of my sight. I walked into the gate with this nigga on my mind and I hoped I didn't give myself up from smiling so hard.

Chapter XXIII

Cash Lopez

BJ's first birthday was two days away and I was scrambling around like a chicken with my head cut off. Even though I had paid help, I had to make sure shit was perfect. Since Paw Patrol was his favorite, we were having every character come out, four jumpers, and everything that came with a carnival. Because of all the things going on, we chose to have it private and at my mother's home. I had just came back from paying the party planner. It was very cloudy so I prayed it wouldn't rain the day of his party. I was now on my way to Trap Gyrl to get my hair done. I wanted to surprise Brook with some faux locks that I knew he would love.

When I pulled up to Trap Gyrl, it looked packed, as always, so I parked in the back. The

TRAP GYRL 3

detail that Brook had, followed behind me, then pulled around back with me. The passenger jumped out and came to open the door for me. He was very handsome and with the description Nina had giving me, I assumed it was him she was crushing on. When I walked in, I made my rounds, saying hi to everyone, and then went to take my seat at Nikki's booth. I knew it would take hours for the style I was getting, so I wanted to hurry and get it over with.

Exactly six hours later, we were done, and it looked better on me than I imagined. I paid her four hundred and she was happy. I kissed her on the check and went into my office. I went over my emails and checked the books for the payments of the week. Satisfied with how much the shop had made, I left and headed to the bank before they closed.

Once I was done for the day, I was tired as hell so I went to my mom's crib to chill with my girls. It was close to seven so I knew that Nina would be back from her boutique. They had been staying at my mother's home for a few months now, and to my surprise, they actually were enjoying them self. I was also happy they were there because they were helping me plan my wedding that was coming up in a few months.

Barbie Scott
TRAP GYRL 3

This time, Brook and I decided to take a yacht with all our guest to the Bahamas. We would have the wedding there and the reception would be on the yacht.

When I walked in the house, I was followed by the cute detail and I knew exactly why. His ass was checking for Nina on the low. On the way here, he asked me a few questions so I knew he was digging her. I informed him that she liked him too, but I made him promise not to tell her I told him.

His name was Morgan aka Money, and the moment she told me she was crushing, I had Marcus do a full background check on him. Of course, he came up clean because he was working for Brooklyn, but I still had to check. Other than him doing service for Brooklyn, he had his hands tied into a gamble shack that was making good money.

"Cash! Oh my God, look at you!" Tiny shouted, the moment she saw me.

"You like it?" I spun around, modeling my hair.

"Yes, I love it."

"Girl, yo' ass fit right in with your big head ass husband and yall big head ass baby," Blaze said laughing.

"Fuck you, Blaze." I laughed with him.

TRAP GYRL 3

Nina emerged from the back and gave me a slight grin. She began running her hand through my locks, pinning them up in the front.

"I love this on you!" she squealed.

I gave her a smirk because I was sure she didn't see Money behind me. When she finally noticed him, her face turned rosy red and she began blushing.

"Hi, Morgan," she smiled, calling him by his government name.

"Sup, sexy," he said, exposing his bottom grill.

I had to give it to Nina, she had taste. He was tall, muscular, and had a handsome face. He looked like he was slightly mixed because of his peanut butter skin tone and tight eyes.

He grabbed her hand and pulled her towards the front of the house, that's when I knew he was about to put his mack down.

"Where's Brook?" I looked over at Blaze.

"That nigga upstairs being Mr. Mom."

"Nigga, you next," I said, and rubbed Tiny's belly. Her ass was now almost five months and she was huge. I guess she took my advice about giving Blaze his first child.

"Yeah, Cash. A nigga bout to be a pappy," he smiled.

TRAP GYRL 3

Right then and there, I was happy she decided to keep it.

After talking to Tiny and Blaze, I went upstairs to find Brooklyn. I walked into my room and Diane looked as if BJ was giving her hell. I chuckled lightly and it made her look up.

"Girl, I don't see how you do it," she said, out of breath. She was trying to get BJ dressed but his little, bad ass was holding her hair with one hand and her necklace with the other. When his eyes fell on me, he let go of her and his face lit up with excitement.

"BJ, you in here giving aunty a hard time, baby," I tickled him and he laughed harder than he already was.

"BJ just reminded me why to never have kids. It took me thirty minutes just to put his pajamas on. Yo baby bad, Cash."

"Awe, Diane. Him just love him aunty," I said, throwing BJ in the air. "Where's Brook?" I asked, and she nodded her head towards the restroom.

When I walked into the restroom, Brook was washing up Braylen. He was talking to him in baby talk and Bray was cracking up laughing. I swear these kids made my day. I loved coming home to BJ and Bray. The way their eyes gleamed every time I walked into the room, warmed my heart. It was like Braylen sensed my presence because he spotted me before Brook.

"Hey, Bray-Bray," I cooed, walking over to the tub.

"Damn, can I get some love," Brook said like he was jealous.

"Awe, daddy. I've missed you too." I pecked his lips.

"Yeah, you getting fucked tonight with this hair do," he said examining my locks.

I smirked and began to blush. It was crazy how all the things we had been through, all the time we've been together, and Brook still made me shy up around him.

"So, I take it you like it?"

"Hell yeah. I love it. This shit look bomb as fuck on you, lil mama."

"Awe, thanks, Big Poppa."

"Braylen's next," he said, referring to Bray getting his hair locked. Even though mine were only temporary, I would love them as long as I had them.

Nina...

Barbie Scott
TRAP GYRL 3

Looking at Morgan was like a breath of the freshest air. His smile was so damn captivating and the way he talked to me caused a throbbing in between my legs. It had been three and a half months since I'd been touched and I needed to get laid in the worst way. I didn't want to move to fast because of Carlos and Dez. However, I did want to get to know Money better. After the bullshit with Carlos, and his cheating, I didn't want to fall in love, so I would put Money on hold until further notice. The one thing I was glad about was that Money was pretty much a part of the empire so I didn't have to worry about any deceitful acts. I knew, right now, he was probably the only nigga I could trust but I would just chill and see where his head was at.

"Nah, baby girl, what you need is a real nigga to hold you down. A lot of niggas don't see your worth but I know what value is, Nina," Money said, knocking me from my thoughts.

"Look, Morgan, I been checking you out and I like what I see. Just from talking to you right now, I could tell that you're a decent guy. However, I've been going through a lot and I don't know if I'm ready to be involved," I said and looked out into the water. We were sitting in Ms. Lopez and Pedro's normal spot and now I see why they always sat here. It had a beautiful view of the home, the pool, and what made it more extravagant was the fifty-foot waterfall. The lighting was so beautiful and It sat the mood for us.

"Look, ma. I ain't tryna rush into nothing. Just give a nigga a chance, though. After I'm done with you, you'll be ready to rock my ring and last name," he said and playfully hit me in the chin. I started blushing, instantly.

"I'm with that." I smiled.

He grabbed my hand and kissed the back of it.

"Bitch, so this why you ain't answering yo' phone?"

Money and I looked up towards the voice.

Here we go with this shit, I thought, and stood to my feet. I was so tired of him, I wished he would just go be happy with whatever bitch he was giving his burnt up ass dick to.

"Nigga, I ain't yo' bitch, and you betta get on, coming over here with that bullshit. I'm not fucking with you no more so get that shit through yo' head, Carlos."

"You gone always be my bitch. And, where the fuck my daughter at while you out here being a hoe."

"My daughter is in the house and in the bed. And, nigga, don't worry about what I do with my pussy."

"Look, ma. I'll see you later."

"No, Money, stay right here, babe."

"Nah, nigga, you might as well get lost before…"

Carlos was cut off by a punch Money connected to his jaw with. I stepped back and let Money do him. If this is what it took for Carlos to know I was done, then so be it.

Carlos stumbled a little and then ran back up on Money, ready to throw down.

Click! The sound of a gun being cocked caught all our attentions.

"You bring this shit to my house, puto. I blow your fucking head off," Ms. Lopez said in her heavy accent. She held the gun steady and looked Carlos dead in his eyes without a single blink.

"Damn, Ms. Lopez, like that?"

"You fucking right. To my understanding, she don't want you so leave her the fuck alone."

By this time, Nino and Cash had rushed outside, followed by Blaze, Tiny, and Diane. Everyone looked on and the looks they wore told

TRAP GYRL 3

Carlos he didn't want it. Carlos looked at everyone and then at me, but I wasn't even fazed by him.

"What's up, Nino?" Carlos said with hopes that Nino would rescue him.

"You heard my mother-in-law, Carlos. Bounce, my nigga," Nino spoke.

At that point, he looked like he lost his best friend. One last look at me, and he walked out without another word. I let out the breath of air I had been holding for what seemed like forever. As much as I didn't want Carlos, I also didn't want Ms. Lopez to blow his wig back. And, that's exactly what she would do.

"You girls gone be the death of me." Ms. Lopez shook her head. "Nina, you and Money, go in the house, Mija. Take him in the room and give him some pinocha because the way you been walking around, it looks like you need to get laid, mi amour," Ms. Lopez said, and we all fell out into laughter. Especially Blaze's ass. He got a kick out of shit like this.

"You good, Money. I let the other guys go home because all the girls are here and nobody's leaving tonight. I'll take you to your car tomorrow," Nino said, and with that, we all walked into the house.

Everyone headed into the game room so we could hit the bar and enjoy the rest of our night. Tonight, I would take Ms. Lopez up on that and take Money into the guest room, that I had been occupying, and give him a piece of my dripping pussy. I mean, after all, the way he handled my baby daddy, that nigga deserved it; not to mention, that shit turned me the fuck on.

Chapter XXIV

Cash Lopez

Brooklyn Carter Jr.'s Birthday Party...

BJ's birthday party is in full effect. He was looking too cute in his custom Paw Patrol two piece Levi outfit. He wore his blue and white Jordan 12's and his locks were fresh. His little jewelry was custom from Marco Brooklyn's jeweler. He bought BJ some baby paw diamond studs, a pendant that read BJ, and two Cuban link chains. My baby was looking like a little GQ baby model.

The sun was out; thank God, but it was still kind of breezy. To my surprise, everyone showed up on time and his gift tables were already filled to capacity. We had twenty guards surrounding the premises and extra sharp shooters on the roof than normal. I couldn't take any chances at my baby's party and especially after all the shit that went down at my wedding.

"Aunty Cash, you look bomb." Cashmere's little-grown butt ran over and said to me. She was only two and a half years old and her little butt was talking too damn good.

"Awww, thank you, niece." I picked her up and kissed her cheek. "You look pretty too. And, I like your hair," I said, grabbing at her one of her long ponytails.

"Tank you." she smiled. "Aunty, yo baby baddd."

"Hahaha. He is, Cashmere?"

"Yeah, he bite me. And hard. I need a band-aid."

"Ok, baby, I'll get you a band-aid."

Barbie Scott
TRAP GYRL 3

"Okay." She smiled and ran off towards the bumper cars.

Brook walked up on me, holding BJ. The party had only been going two hours and my baby looked so tired already. I took him from Brook and headed over to the tents where Blaze and Tiny were sitting. I needed to rest my feet because I hadn't sat down once this morning.

"Look at these two." Tiny smiled, looking in the direction of the door.

I looked where she was looking and Nina and Money were all in each other's personal space. Nina was smiling from ear to ear and Money had one hand wrapped around her waist. I had to admit, they looked so cute together.

"Hiii, nephew!" Breelah shouted, taking BJ out my arms. She then kissed me on the cheek and continued to play with BJ.

"Hey, Que." I stood up to greet him.

"Sup, Wifee," he said, smiling. No one seemed to pay it any mind because they knew that would forever be my pet name. He didn't care, he would call me that in front of Bree or Brook and didn't give two fucks what anyone thought.

Que then handed me a bag with five jewelry boxes. I was too damn anxious, so I opened them.

215

TRAP GYRL 3

"For real, Que," I said, laughing.

This nigga had gotten my baby a custom diamond Rolex watch, some BJ earrings, a Rolex chain, and what really tripped me out was the diamond grill. The moment I saw it, I raised it in the air so everyone could see. We all started laughing.

"I told that fool don't get that damn grill, Cash. I mean, it's bad enough he has a Rolex. What one-year-old you know that has a Rolex?" Breelah said, and again, we all laughed.

"Bree, your ass ain't no better, ma. I saw that damn customized Maybach. What, you thought that big ass box was hidden?"

I laughed and playfully nudged her shoulder.

Breelah and Que headed inside the house to eat. It was time BJ had some fun because I was trying to keep him woke as long as possible. Tiny grabbed Bray from Brooklyn and we went on our way over to the bumper cars.

After riding every last ride with the babies, we headed towards the cake table to begin cutting the cake. Tiny announced to the kids that it was time and they bum-rushed us for the delicious sweets. After the last kid got their cake, I was ready to open the gifts. I called Brook over to hold BJ so I could start opening them. Before I could even grab the first box, we heard screaming and a loud commotion going on inside the home. My mother and father were in the house so that was what had me nervous. Whoever it was, they would most likely not make it, I just prayed it was nothing serious.

Brook and I ran inside the house and when we made it further inside, I was shocked to see, "Carter?" I asked like I had seen a ghost.

The tension was so heavy, I didn't know rather to be scared or embrace him.

"Hey, Car..."

Before I could finish, Que pulled out his gun. Right on cue, Carter whipped out his pistol also. I didn't know what the hell was going on but I knew it damn sure didn't have anything to do with me.

"Nigga, I ought to blow yo' fucking head off," Que yelled with his gun aiming at Carter.

"Do it, bitch ass nigga!" Carter spoke with so much vengeance in his voice.

"What the hell is going on?" I asked, almost in tears. This was my right-hand man and my brother-in-law ready to kill each other.

"Man, y'all niggas wilding, yo," Brooklyn said, stepping in between the two. "Que, you not about to kill my brother in front of me, my nigga. So, put the strap down or shit is gonna get ugly," Brooklyn said, ready to reach for his gun as well.

"Nah, Nino, this nigga foul as fuck." Que looked at Brook. "Yeah, tell this nigga you the one that shot us," Que said with his gun still drawn.

What the fuck is he talking about? I thought as I watched on.

"Yeah, this nigga is the one that shot me and Bree."

It was like the moment he said that time froze. The sound of Breelah weeping made me look into her direction. Carter, who stood there with a clenched jaw, looked like he was ready to kill Que at any moment.

"Is that true, Carter," I asked with a stream of tears. I couldn't believe what I was hearing.

"I'm so sorry, Bree," Carter said, looking at his sister. "I didn't know you were in the car, ma, I swear."

"But, why?" I asked Carter through a tear stained face.

"This the nigga that shot me when I hid out for those five years. Yeah, I bet he didn't tell y'all his punk ass was working with the Cartel," Carter said.

Everyone now focused their attention on Que.

Barbie Scott
TRAP GYRL 3

"Nigga, I did not work for them. That shit was personal with me."

"What, because yo' hoe ass was in love with Cash? You wanted me dead that bad, my nigga?" Carter said and it all started to make sense.

I thought back to how Que was acting when Carter had first died. He did not show a sign of remorse and he acted strangely the moment Carter resurfaced. I also remembered a time when they came face to face and were ready to draw their guns on one another.

"Daddy!" Britt screamed, running to Carter. When she realized what was going on, she looked between the two and her smile turned into fear. Que was ready to shoot Carter and Carter wore the same expression.

"So, y'all gone do this shit in front of all these kids?" I asked, looking from Que to Carter. "Just go, Que!" I yelled, but they both weren't budging.

"Y'all niggas got ten seconds to get the fuck away from my home with this shit. It's my grandson's birthday and I think y'all forgot who house y'all was in. Now, if y'all want, I could have my shooters come in and body both you pendejos," my mother said, walking further to where they stood.

Barbie Scott
TRAP GYRL 3

The roar of her voice seemed to have shaken the entire room. I was so caught up in my feelings about the whole situation, I grabbed BJ and Bray, and headed upstairs. Them niggas could kill each other for all I cared. This shit was just a bit too much for me.

Chapter XXV
Que

While, standing in front of this nigga Carter, it took everything in me not to blow this nigga wig back. Had we been in a different environment, I would have done just that. Even with his daughter standing there, I would have still shot his ass right where he stood. The only thing saved him was Ms. Lopez. I wasn't worried about her killing me because death is one thing I did not fear. However, she had done so much for me and I didn't want to disrespect her home. I hated shit had to go down like this, but I knew eventually, it would have happened.

Seeing Cash storm off with tears in her eyes killed me. I ran behind her because I knew I had shit to explain so I would catch this nigga at a later date. I didn't give a fuck if Nino wanted in on this, I had a few bullets with that nigga name on it too.

When I walked into Cash's room, she was sitting on the bed crying her eyes out. I took a deep breath and walked in, closing the door behind me. She didn't bother to look at me once. I stood there, froze, not knowing what to say but I knew I had to say something.

"Look, Wifee, I'm sorry this shit had to go down like this. Especially at BJ's party. Sooner or later, I'ma kill that nigga and I just hope you forgive me."

"Have you lost your damn mind, Quintin?" she shot me a look with so much hatred. When she called me by my government name, I knew she was mad.

"That nigga almost killed me and his own fucking sister, ma." I tried to reason with her.

"But, you started this shit. You tried to kill him first. What's crazy is, you sat in my face all those years knowing you were behind that shit. Not to mention, you sat in his face, and his brothers face after it was all said and done. And, oh, poor Breelah. We not even gonna mention how you tried to kill him first and now you're fucking his sister! Are you fucking crazy!" she shouted.

"Man, it wasn't even..." she cut me off.

"Just get the fuck out, Que."

"But, Wifee..."

"Don't wifee me, shit. All this madness is your fault. You started all this over some fucking pussy. Some fucking pussy that would never be yours. I mean, think about it, Que. If I wanted to be with you, I would have married you, instead of Brook. I didn't want you then and I don't want you now! So please, just leave me the fuck alone, for good. Any more business, you could handle that shit with my mother. I'm through with yo' snake ass."

After all the harsh words, I couldn't do shit but shake my head. I took one last look at her and walked out the door. The look on her face told me she wasn't playing and that shit broke the last part of the heart I had left.

I walked downstairs and it was like the whole house mugged me. Ms. Lopez didn't say shit, Esco didn't say shit. Even Blaze, Tiny, and Nina was on hush. I looked at Bree and she still had tears in her eyes. I didn't know if I should call out to her or what. She tried her hardest to not look at me but fuck that, this was my bitch.

"You rolling or what, Bree?" I asked her, pretty much knowing the answer.

"Nigga, she ain't going nowhere with you," Carter shot at me.

I let that little shit slide and looked at Bree to see her reaction. When she didn't budge, I took it as she was also turning her back on me.

Barbie Scott
TRAP GYRL 3

I walked out the front door and didn't bother to look back.

Fuck everybody, I thought as I walked to my ride.

When I hopped in, I turned on my 2Pac CD and went straight to the song I felt was for me at that moment.

> *It's just me against the world*
> *Ooh, ooh*
> *Nothin' to lose,*
> *It's just me against the world, baby*
> *Oh, ah ah*
> *I got nothin' to lose*
> *It's just me against the world*
> *Oh-hahhh*
> *Stuck in the game*
> *Me against the world, baby*

Bumping "Me Against the World" had a nigga in his feelings. Right now, I didn't have anybody. Keisha was in rehab, Qui was in the system, Stephanie was dead, the Cartel had my baby that I never got to see, Cash had just scratched me out her life, and Breelah had just shitted on me. It was like I couldn't win for losing. I decided to just go home so

Barbie Scott
TRAP GYRL 3

I could cuddle up with a bottle of Hennessy. The only thing that ever helped me out in a situation was some pussy, but the way I was feeling, I didn't even want to be bothered with no bitches. Tonight, I would go to bed with a million thoughts and try to figure out my next move. I was so tired at this point, I wanted to just move the fuck away and start over. I had enough money to get out the game and tonight, I would give it much thought.

A few days later…

I woke up with a cold ass hangover. I stayed up all night, every night, drinking my life away. It had been three days since the shit with Carter and not one muthafucka called to see how I was feeling; not even Breelah. I lifted out of bed and went to take a shower and brush my grill. After I was done, I slid on a gray Nike jogger set and headed out the door. I had someone to see and just prayed this shit wouldn't go sour.

When I pulled up, I bounced out and went inside. I signed my name on the list and took a seat outside. It was a gated fenced like they had in prison, decorated with rose bushes. The sun was shining bright and it felt good to be away from

Barbie Scott
TRAP GYRL 3

Miami. Even though I was only a few miles out, everything seemed so different. The air, the atmosphere, and even the people that walked past. I was still caught up in my thoughts so I dropped my head into my hands and braced myself.

"Que?"

I looked up and her angelic voice took me down memory lane. I don't know if it was because I didn't have anyone by my side or did I really miss her, but she looked good as the day she did when I first met her. She was wearing her real shoulder length hair and she had gotten thicker than before. Her face was now blemished free and she looked good and healthy.

"Sup, Keish?" I smiled at my daughter's mother.

She stood frozen, not believing it was really me, and that shit really made me feel like shit. I loved Keisha so much but I was so caught up over Cash's ass, I never realized it. Cash was right, if she wanted me, then she would have been with me. Even though the signs were there, I never paid attention.

"Awe, baby daddy." Keisha ran up and gave me a strong hug. I hugged her back, tightly, and it was like I never wanted to let her go.

Barbie Scott
TRAP GYRL 3

When we broke our embrace, she instantly began to cry.

"I'm so sorry, Que. I swear, I never meant…"

I put my finger up to her mouth to keep her from talking. I knew she was sorry for what had happened, and now was the time to forgive her.

"It's straight, ma. I know I was the cause for a lot of this shit. Don't cry, baby girl, we gone fix this shit, alright?"

She shook her head up and down, but she couldn't stop crying.

"Qui is straight, Keish. I go to court next month and I promise I'ma get her back, ma. Once you get out of here, we gone leave Miami and move away somewhere, aight?" I said, wiping her tears away.

"Are you serious? We're really gonna go?" she asked, unsure.

"I'm dead ass, baby. We out this muthafucka. Ain't shit here for us."

"So, where we gonna go?"

"Brazil," was all I said and shook my head up and down. "You hungry?"

"Yeah, a little. The food here is ok, but I miss the outside food."

"Alright, go grab your shit. Tell them you only leaving for a few hours, okay?"

TRAP GYRL 3

"Ok," she said and rose to her feet.

When she walked into the facility, I placed the call that I had been waiting on for what seemed like a lifetime.

"Hello, Papi."

"Sup, ma? Everything green over there?"

"Yeah, Papi. green light."

"Aight, it's time. Handle that and call me when it's done."

"Done deal." And, with that, we disconnected the line.

When Keish came back out, I grabbed her hand and led her out towards my ride. I had big plans for us and I wouldn't let her down on my promise. Brazil would be our new residence soon.

Chapter XXVI

Bronx Carter

I really hated how that nigga Que tried to expose me to the fam by saying I was behind the shooting. Even though they understood I didn't mean to shoot my little sister, she still seemed mad at me. Breelah wouldn't talk to me and Nino was giving me the cold shoulder. I wanted to kill that nigga so bad, I could taste it. The only thing that saved his ass was Britt running into the house. I didn't give a fuck about Ms. Lopez killing me, as long as I got the first shot on Que, I was fine with that. And, that's how bad I wanted that nigga dead.

After everything happened that day, Lydia had been ignoring my ass. She even went as far as to taking the kids and going to stay at her mother's house. She kept telling me she was at a hotel but little did she know, I had already followed her a couple of times. The only reason I didn't expose her fake ass story was because I needed to get back home, make sure Gabriela was straight, and then I would be going back to Miami for a few months. Cash and Nino were having another wedding, and this time, I couldn't miss that shit. I, at least, owed that to my brother.

When I got off my private jet, Gabriela was right there waiting for me, like always. I swear I owed this girl my life. For so long, she knew I didn't love her and she also knew my heart was still with Cash's ass. She accepted it and sucked that shit up. Now, with all the madness going on, I felt like Gabriela was the only loyal one in my corner. It had been many times I contemplated marrying her. Yes, I was already married but that was in Miami. Shit, it was a whole other ball game in another country.

By the time we made it to my mansion, I was tired as fuck from my long flight. All I wanted was a hot shower, a good meal, and some of Gabriela's warm tight pussy. While in Miami, I was hoping to taste Lydia's cookie jar but she wasn't fucking with a nigga.

Walking into my room, I went straight to the shower. The water was so hot, it had the entire bathroom fogged up from the steam. I stepped in and let the water run over my entire body, locks, and all. A nigga's head was really fucked up with all types of thoughts but the hot water relaxed me and put my mind at ease.

"Can I join you?" Gabriela asked me with her sexy ass accent. She was naked as the day she was born, and damn, her body was banging. I swear, if I didn't know any better, I would think she spent a million dollars on her body but that shit was natural. She didn't have any kids and she didn't miss a day of a hard workout.

"Hell yeah. Bring that ass here."

She stepped into the shower and took her position. She dropped right to her knees and took my dick all the way in her mouth. I'm talking about touching her tonsils. That was what really made me love her. She could swallow my dick whole and a nigga was working with a mandingo.

"Shit, girl!"

She had me screaming out like a hoe. She slurped, sucked, and even licked my balls while my dick was still in her mouth. I grabbed her head and pumped in and out her mouth like I was fucking her pussy. I knew, sooner or later, I would bust a fat ass nut, and like always, she would swallow every drop.

***

Barbie Scott
TRAP GYRL 3

After that fire ass head job I got from Gabriela, a nigga was starving. I headed downstairs to see what she was whipping up. She had the whole house smelling good as fuck and that shit only made me hungrier. This girl knew she could burn.

I walked into the kitchen and hugged her around her waist. She turned around and kissed me like she loved me to death. When I broke our kiss, I smacked her on the ass and took my seat at the dinner table. She brought me my plate with a bottle of Ace of Spade. She poured my glass for me then headed back into the kitchen, I assumed, to, get her plate. When she came back, she took her seat and without another word, we dove in. I scarfed my food down with the quickness. Once I was halfway done, I downed the glass of champagne then poured another glass. I was full as a muthafucka so I slid the plate from in front of me. All I wanted to do was get drunk, ease my mind, and go round for round in Gabby's pretty pussy.

I downed the second cup of champagne and just that fast, I felt a slight buzz. Gabriela was eyeing me the entire time so she must have seen how faded I was getting so quickly. She was still eating her food and not saying much of nothing. I refilled my glass for the third time and when I put

TRAP GYRL 3

the glass to my lips to drink, it was like my whole
body locked up on me. The glass slipped out my
hand and hit the floor. My head began to spin and I
started choking. It was like my throat had locked up
and I wasn't getting any air. I grabbed my throat
and tried calling out to Gabby. My vision was
blurring but I saw her reach over and grab her
phone.

"It done," was all she said and hung up the
phone.

*Do this bitch not see me over here damn near
dying?* I thought as my head started spinning
profoundly.

"Gab… Gab… help. Call…" It was like I
couldn't get the words out.

She was just sitting there watching me, and
that's when it hit me. This bitch had poisoned me. I
was on the verge of catching my last breath. I could
feel my eyes rolling to the back of my head. I tried
my hardest to catch my breath but wasn't shit
working. Tired of fighting, I just laid on the floor,
still. My heart rate sped up and I knew my life way
over. I tried to call out to her again but failed. I
drifted into a dark place and I knew now, it was
over. I took my last breath and then walked into the
gates of heaven.

Chapter XXVII

Brooklyn Nino

The wedding was one week away, and I couldn't wait. After all the bullshit that had been going on, marrying Cash would be the only thing to make me happy. After our first wedding not going good, we decided to just hop on a yacht and do it big in the Bahamas. We made sure to keep the wedding immediate. My crew, Cash's crew, and our family. Nobody had heard from Que, so I guess he wouldn't be attending. I was mad as fuck at him and Bronx, but this day meant a lot to Cash, and Que was a part of the circle.

He and Bronx were on some stupid shit, trying to kill each other, and I would say they were even. Que was foul for the shit he pulled years ago, but Bronx was wrong too. This nigga almost killed our little sister over this bullshit. To think about it, right

234

TRAP GYRL 3

before I was about to walk down the aisle with Cash, he had called crying saying he fucked up but I shut him out, selfishly. It was my big day and I didn't need anything else fucking it up. Tiffany had already called, talking about she was pregnant so whatever Bronx had going on, at that moment, I didn't care.

Speaking of Bronx, I had been calling that nigga for the last month and he hadn't answered. I guess he was still in his feelings too. It was weird, though, because no matter what, that nigga would always answer his phone. I had even reached out to his little Brazilian bitch and she said he hadn't been there since he had come to Miami. Lydia didn't know where he was at. I just prayed he didn't do any dumb shit.

I had Marcus searching all the hospitals and jails around the world and he didn't show up in not one system. I had so much to do before the wedding so I pretty much gave up looking. I knew eventually he would surface. I just hoped he would at least show up to my wedding, being that he missed the first one.

The sound of my phone broke me from my trance. I looked at the caller ID and it was my baby.

"Sup, stink?"

TRAP GYRL 3

"Hey, daddy. You miss me?"

"Hell yeah, ma. What yo' ass doing out there, you bet not be hooking up with one of those Cali niggas."

"I'm trying to get back to you, daddy. Where's BJ? I miss you guys."

"He in the guest room with Rosa."

"Oh, okay. Well, I'll be home in two days. I love you."

"Yeah, you and Nina bet not make me fuck y'all up. I love you too, ma."

We hung up the phone.

I didn't understand women one bit. Cash flew her ass out to Cali just for some damn hair. All that hair she had, and she wanted a damn weave. Hey, it was her big day so whatever she wanted to make her happy, it was hers.

I went to the guest room to check on Rosa and BJ and let them know that I would be heading out. I was looking fresh to death and since my wife was out and about, it wasn't any sense in me sitting in the house, all lonely and shit. After playing with BJ for a while, I headed out the house to go scoop my nigga Money. Since Nina was gone, he wanted to get out too, so we were going to hit the strip club and enjoy our night.

Barbie Scott
TRAP GYRL 3

***

Club Wet was in full effect. We sat in our VIP section and took down bottle after bottle. We got a few lap dances but nothing major. It was crazy how these hoes were going crazy over us. I guess since Cash wasn't with me, they figured it was a green light. Every bitch in this club feared Cash, they wouldn't even look my way when she was with me.

I looked over at Money, who was getting a lap dance, and he seemed to not be enjoying it. I couldn't help but laugh because that nigga was missing Nina. I couldn't say I didn't blame him because I was missing Cash's ass too.

"Not one bitch in this club got shit on our bitches, Money," I looked over and said, as soon as the chick left from giving him a dance.

He shook his head in agreement and we both fell out laughing.

"I wonder what they ass doing?" he smirked.

"Man, I know they better be sleep or I'ma fuck both they ass up."

We laughed again.

"Fuck that, I'm about to Facetime her," Money said, sounding thirsty as hell.

TRAP GYRL 3

He pulled his phone out and dialed the number. After a shit load of rings, Nina's ass finally answered. She was screaming so loud, I heard her from where I was sitting.

"Hey, babe."

"Sup, ma? What yo' ass doing?"

"We're at a club for a performance. Chick name Barbie Amor performing. Cash wanna bring her to Miami and start a record label."

"Oh, is that right? So, y'all out shaking y'all ass, huh?"

"No, nigga. And, where you at? While you talking 'bout me."

"Club...."

"Oh, is that right. And, who you with?" Nina asked.

I looked into the phone and did a little dance, letting her know it was ya boy.

"Ooh, I'm telling. Cash!" she called out, and me and Money fell out laughing.

Cash jumped her ass right into the camera with a smirk.

"Don't make us hop on a plane, tonight, and fuck y'all up, Nino," Cash said.

"We ain't doing shit baby. These hoes are dry. All we doing is having a drink and we're leaving."

TRAP GYRL 3

"Yeah, ok, muthafucka."

"While y'all talking, where the fuck y'all at?"

"Huh? I can't hear you," she lied. She passed Nina back the phone and that shit really had us laughing.

"A'ight, baby, we gotta go. We bout to get some lap dances," Money said and hung up. Before the phone disconnected, Nina's face flushed with anger and that shit was hella funny.

"Man, you tryna get us killed.

After about twenty minutes, two security guards walked to our VIP and stood right in the front. A few strippers tried to get in our section but security turned them away. I looked over with a what the fuck look, then stood to my feet. I walked over to the guards to see what the fuck was up.

"Man, what's up with y'all. Why y'all turning the ladies away?"

"We have strict orders not to let any women in, Nino. Nothing personal."

"What the fuck? And, who those orders from? Sam," I asked, referring to the owner.

"Sam don't have anything to do with this."

"So, who the fuck sent y'all?"

"Cash Lopez," one of the guards said.

TRAP GYRL 3

"Cash?" *What type of shit is this?* I thought, laughing.

"How much is she paying y'all?" I smirked while Money was on the side of me cracking up.

"Ten g's each."

I couldn't help but laugh. Cash's ass was crazy as fuck. This damn girl was too much. I reached into my pockets and pulled out my bankroll.

"Well look, here go ten more g's to act like y'all ain't saw shit."

Money also reached into his pockets and pulled out another ten g's. We handed them the money and them niggas stepped to the side. I knew with these niggas, money talked. But to keep it one hunnit, it wasn't even about the money, it was because Cash Lopez had said so.

Money and I went back over to our sofa and took a seat. This shit was so funny, we couldn't stop laughing. For the rest of the night, we chilled and got a couple more dances. It was close to two in the morning, so soon, we would be leaving.

Chapter XXVIII

Cash Lopez & Nina

"Ooh, Cash, now you know you wrong," Nina laughed.

"Fuck that, ma. Them niggas got us fucked up."

We both laughed.

I knew I was being petty, but I wanted to show Brook that no matter where I was, I had shit on lock. I wasn't really tripping off him because, after all, the begging and pleading he did during our breakup, I trusted him. Not to mention, he murdered his own baby mother to get our family back intact. So again, I trusted him.

"She did good, Cash," Nina said, referring to the artist Barbie Amor who had just gotten off the stage.

"Hell yeah. Her ass dope as fuck. I really wanna get her to Miami and possibly sign her. Shit, I'll buy a studio and get her plugged with the radio stations."

Barbie Scott
TRAP GYRL 3

"Yeah, she would kill in Miami."

Nina and I were having the time of our life in California. We had come out here so I could purchase some hair from my girl, KitKat, for my wedding. She had the best hair in the country and I was so desperate, I flew all the way to Cali for six bundles. People always said that we looked alike, and no lie, she was bomb as fuck.

I pulled out my iPhone and typed @Hairbykitkat in the search bar to show Nina her hair. I knew that once she laid her eyes on the 30 inch Brazilian, she would most definitely want to purchase a few bundles for herself.

Once we left the club, we headed to our hotel on Rodeo Drive, called the Beverly-Wilshire Hotel. Just our hotel alone made me consider moving out to Cali. I knew that I would be out here more often because Brook was opening another restaurant here. They had great weather, just like at home, and the best strips to shop. When we walked into our rooms, Nina went to hers and I went to mine. I wanted to call Brook but I didn't want him to think I was blocking his fun, so I chose against it and went to take my shower.

Once I was done, I slipped into something comfortable and went downstairs to drink. The atmosphere was nice and soothing. A guy in a white tuxedo played the piano and an older white lady was singing. The lighting was beautiful and everyone seemed so friendly. I took a seat at the wet bar and waved the tender over. I placed an order for a double shot of Hennessy XO and a glass of Dom Perignon.

"Sup, sexy?" I heard a masculine voice behind me.

When I turned around in my chair, I was taken by surprise when he presented me with his handsome face. His fade was on point, his gear was fresh to death, and his jewelry lit up the entire room. He had a cute baby face but I could tell wasn't anything baby about him.

"Hi." I smiled shyly.

He waved the bartender over and placed an order of Ace of Spade champagne. He took a seat beside me and shot me a sexy ass grin. I know I had no business checking the guy out, but this man was fine as hell.

"So, what's up with you. You enjoying yourself?"

"Well, yeah. I'm just relaxing."

"What's yo' name? If you don't mind me asking."

"Cash."

"Oh, okay. I'm Jay." He extended his hand.

"Can I get a number on you or something?"

"Well, I'm... I'm married." I stumbled over my words.

He chuckled a little bit before responding.

"Well, I figured that, as sexy as your ass is."

"Thank you." I blushed. "Do you have an Instagram or something? I mean, we could be friends."

"Yeah. Add me. It's el_segundoboy."

I pulled my phone out and added him. I looked over a few of his pictures and he was indeed hot. Every pic, he was dressed to a tee, and I could tell he was enjoying life.

"You from out here in Cali?"

"Yeah. You?"

"No, I'm from Miami."

"Oh, okay. That's what's up."

"Aye, E, we booked in, let's roll," a guy walked up and said.

He stood to his feet and shot me his dimple.

"I gotta bounce, ma. But make sure you hit me up sometimes."

"Okay. I will do," I replied and he walked off.

His walk was so demanding and I watched him until he was out of eyes view.

Damn, I thought and let out a deep breath. *If this what these niggas in Cali looked like, then I need to stay my ass home.*

After finishing my drink, I headed back up to my room. I was now drunk and horny, so I would be Facetiming Brook for an over the camera session.

***

Nina...

I couldn't wait to get back home to Money. Don't get me wrong, I had a ball in Cali, but I needed some dick. It was like I was craving his touch. Lately, we had been kicking it tough and I felt myself falling for him more and more. I hadn't seen him since I'd been back because our flight got in late and I was tired as ever.

When I woke up this morning, I headed straight to my boutique to get some work done. When I walked in, it was a little busy for it to have been so early in the morning. I went to my office and began fumbling through paperwork. The door opened and

TRAP GYRL 3

it was my worker, telling me Money was in the front asking for me. I smiled so wide, I made her chuckle. I told her to send him back and she closed the door behind herself. I tried my hardest to act like I wasn't excited, so I quickly wiped the smile away. He walked in, looking sexy as ever, and by the smile on his face, he was happy to see me as well.

"Sup, sexy?"

"Hey, baby." I stood up and hugged him.

"You missed a nigga?"

"Hell yeah, I did."

"I came to holla at you about some shit." He looked off into space as if something was weighing heavy on his mind.

"What is that?" I took my seat back behind my desk.

"Well, a nigga been thinking heavy, ma. Like, what are we doing? Where is this relationship going?"

Oh, boy, I thought to myself and began fidgeting in my seat.

"I mean, shit, we're doing great. So, what's on your mind?"

"Are you ready to make this shit official?"

"I guess so." I bit my bottom lip.

TRAP GYRL 3

"What you mean *you guess*? Are you rocking with the kid or what?"

"Yes, Morgan, I'm rocking with you."

"So, that means you're my girl, right?"

"Yes." I smiled.

I wanted this relationship just as bad as him. I had been through so much in my life, I needed to be genuinely loved, and Money was the one who was loving me. I didn't know how long the relationship would last, but right now, it felt so right.

"I love yo' ass already," he said and shook his head.

I didn't respond. Not because I didn't love him, but because I was shocked as hell he said it.

He walked over to me and in one swift move, he picked me up out my chair and sat me on my desk. He looked me in my eyes and said, "You hear me, Nina? A nigga love you, ma," he said without giving me a chance to respond.

He then kissed me so passionately, I lost focus of everything I was doing. He broke the kiss and slid my skirt up aggressively. He began massaging my clit with his finger and that shit had me moaning out in pure ecstasy. He dropped his pants, followed by his briefs, and stood before him stroking his manhood. My love box was dripping like a faucet. I pulled at his dick and guided him inside of me. He hit me with nice slow strokes, and for the first time, we did it without a condom.

Damn, I hope I don't get pregnant.

We were so caught up in the moment, we never heard the door open. When we looked over, Carlos was standing there with a look of disgust. His eyes began to water and like a bitch, this nigga was straight crying. Money wasn't making things any better because he stroked my pussy a few more times and then pulled out of me with a slight smirk.

"Handle that," he said and picked up his clothes and headed into my bathroom.

"So, I guess it's really over, huh?" Carlos said, sounding brokenhearted. I hated he had to see this, but shit, what was I supposed to do? I mean, I was in my own space.

"I'm sorry, Carlos." I shook my head and now my eyes began to water.

I wasn't crying because I still loved him, I was hurt because I hated the fact that I couldn't get rid of this nigga. I didn't want him any longer and I wished he would just realize it. Now look, he walked in as my new man made love to me and I knew it was like a stab in the heart.

TRAP GYRL 3

He turned to walk away but I didn't want him to leave like this. I really wanted to have a real heart to heart with him and let him know what it was.

"Wait, Carlos." I jumped from my desk and quickly put on my clothing.

Before I could get my clothing on, he had already walked out, feeling defeated. I turned around and Money was eying me with a pained look.

"You still love that nigga, huh?" he asked with so much force.

"No, Money, I don't. It's just…"

I was cut off.

"So, what the fuck you crying for, Nina?" he asked, looking upset.

I couldn't even respond because it was too much to explain. With one last look, he shook his head and walked out the door without another word.

Fuck! I cursed myself and for the first time, I wished I was still in Cali.

***

Three days had gone by, and Money hadn't called or bother to respond to a single text. After the second day, I had stopped calling because I wasn't

about to be made a fool. No lie, I was stressed out
because he wasn't giving me a chance to explain,
but I wasn't kissing any ass. I mean, he needed to
understand, Carlos was Cashmere's father and he
would always be around. However, my heart was
now with him and I really planned to make it work.

Tired of sitting in the house, I got dressed and
went downstairs. I tried to sneak past Nino but he
wasn't having it.

"Where yo' ass think you going, Nina?"

Shit. I thought, and turned around.

"I'm going to the mall, Nino. Can a girl live?"

"Yeah, you could live with the security," he
chuckled.

He placed a call to the detail and I prayed it
wasn't Money that would be driving me. When
Nino smirked, I knew exactly what his ass was up
too.

"They'll be here in fifteen minutes," he smiled
and walked towards the back of the home.

I was still staying at Ms. Lopez's house, in not
only fear of the Cartel, but Carlos' ass too. Nino and
Cash had also been staying here, but Diane had left
out of town for work. She would be back the
morning of the wedding so I was pretty much left
alone. Cash was busy planning her wedding, Tiny's

pregnant ass was home with Blaze, and of course, Ms. Lopez was with Esco. *Damn, I missed Niya.*

Exactly fifteen minutes later, the detail was outside waiting for me. I walked towards the van and could only shake my head. When I hopped in the back, Money didn't bother to say one word to me. I sat back, quietly, and made the best out of my ride.

When we pulled up to the mall, they parked the van and got out. I looked at them like they were crazy because I didn't need their ass babysitting me while I shopped. I needed to buy something for Cashmere to wear to the wedding, and I was going to make sure I took my precious time.

"Damn, I don't need y'all babysitting me while I shop." I stopped walking and put my hands on my hips.

"We can't leave yo ass, ma. Strict orders," Jason, the driver, said and walked to the door.

I pouted like a seven-year-old child as I made my way inside.

I went to a few stores and just that fast, I was exhausted. I had to make one more stop in Saks so I could get Cashmere's hair accessories. Speaking of the devil, she was Facetiming me from Cash's phone. I answered, and I couldn't help but smile at her little cute self.

"Hcy, Cashy."

"Hi, mommy," she smiled.

"When did you get there?"

"Daddy just brought me now."

"Oh, okay. Well, I'm at the mall getting your dress for Cash's wedding."

"Yayy. Pink, you got me pink?"

"Yes, baby, I got you pink."

"Who you with, mommy? Money?" she asked, and I couldn't help but laugh. This girl was too damn smart.

"I'm with Money, baby," I responded, and looked over to make sure he had heard Cashmere ask.

When he wasn't standing beside me, I began to search the store. I spotted him outside the door and my face flushed with anger. He was talking to some chick and that shit had me 38-hot.

"I'll see you in a minute, Cashy, okay?"

"Okay, mommy," she saidand blew me a kiss. I blew her a kiss back and disconnected the call. I stormed over to Money and the girl, furiously.

"You really got me fucked up, Morgan."

"Man, Nina, gone with that shit, ma."

Barbie Scott
TRAP GYRL 3

"Oh, gone with that shit? Do you mean that?" I asked with force because, on some real shit, I really would be *gone with that shit* and fall all the way back. He's the one that asked to be with me, so shit, I wasn't pressed for a relationship.

"You heard him," the bitch had the audacity to say.

It was like I blacked out because I two-pieced the bitch with a side of potatoes and the gravy. The bitch didn't even get a chance to swing back, and next thing I know, I was being snatched off her. Jason held me off my feet all the way outside of the mall. I didn't even bother to look at Money as I got into the van. This nigga had me all the way fucked up.

When we got back to the mansion, I stormed upstairs to my room, still mad as fuck. I sat my bags down and began taking off my clothing so I could slide into something a little more relaxing. This nigga had fucked up my whole day. After the mall, I was supposed to go let Nikki hook my hair up, then I was going to grab some lobster and cheese bread.

"Man, all that wasn't even called for, Nina," Money said, walking into my room.

"Just leave me alone, Morgan." I walked into the restroom.

TRAP GYRL 3

"Is that what you want me to do?"

"Nigga, that's what you wanted me to do at the mall. You played me to the left, for a bitch," I shouted and tears came down my face. My feelings weren't hurt, I was crying because I was mad as fuck.

"I'm sorry, ma. A nigga was on some dumb shit. But, Nina, you can't control shit around me, when you the one that's caught up in a love triangle."

"I'm not caught up in shit!"

"Don't raise yo voice at me, ma," he said, and I knew he wasn't playing.

"I had just made you my bitch and you sitting here crying over the next nigga. Not to mention, I heard you call out for the nigga when he was leaving. How the fuck you think I felt? You're my bitch. Don't ever disrespect me and call out for the next nigga."

"It wasn't like that," I said and dropped my head.

He used his hand to lift my chin and made me look at him.

"Look, ain't no need to explain shit, Nina. If you rocking with me, then you rocking with me. Whatever feelings you got for that nigga, you need

TRAP GYRL 3

to dead that shit or next time it's gonna be a real issue." He looked at me and I could tell the feelings he had for me were still there.

I shook my head, yes, and it was like I fell putty in his hands. He kissed me, passionately, and right then and there, I knew we would be finishing what we had started in my office.

Chapter XXIX

Breelah Carter

It was the day of my brother and Cash's wedding, and I hadn't heard from Que or talked to him. I knew he was mad because I didn't leave with him the day he and Carter got into it. I mean, damn, he was too stubborn to understand that I was stuck between a rock and a hard place. That's my damn brother. In my eyes, they both were wrong, but I prayed they could just leave this shit alone so we could move on with our lives. I guess that was wishful thinking because the way they looked at each other one last time, I knew this shit was far from over.

Since Que and I were pretty much done, Brook thought it was best I go stay in Ms. Lopez's house with Nina and Diane, but I refused. I had gone to stay at my condo near campus and he agreed to let me go. Staying at Ms. Lopez's house would have been a bit too much for me so I opted out.

Barbie Scott
TRAP GYRL 3

My flight landed back in Miami this morning so I was now at Ms. Lopez's home, getting ready to board the yacht to the Bahamas. Every day, I missed Que so much. I prayed he would at least show his face at the wedding. I needed him in the worst way. I wanted to tell him I loved him and not only that, I was pregnant. Yes, I'm prego and for the first time ever in my life. I was keeping it from my brothers because I knew they would kill me but I knew, sooner or later, they would find out. I contemplated getting an abortion but thought against it because this could be my only chance at motherhood; you never know.

I pulled out my phone and shot Que a text. I knew he wouldn't respond, but I hoped he would at least get the message.

Me: *I just wanted to tell you I love you and I really miss you. Today's the wedding so I hope and pray I see you there so we could talk.*

After I sent the text, I went into the restroom to begin my shower.

Once I stepped in, I let the hot water soothe me. I was so caught up in my feelings, I began to cry, silently. Everything that was going on was taking a toll on me. From the shit with my brother and Que, to the whole Cartel thing. For the first time, I wished I would have never come back home from college because I was now with child and a broken-hearted girl.

I began to lather my towel, and when it was good and soapy, I washed up and hopped out. I went into the room and began getting dress. The color theme for the wedding was silver, so I bought a silver David Koma bodycon dress and some Rodarte ankle boots. My hair was in a sleek ponytail to the back with a part down the middle and my baby hairs were slicked to the gods. Once I was done dressing, I went downstairs to get my makeup done by the Mac makeup artist Brook had hired for me and the girls. Cash was getting her makeup done on the boat and was also dressing on the boat, as well.

"Check baby sis out," Brook said, grabbing my hand to spin me around.

I faintly smiled and walked over to take my seat.

Nina was in the chair, so I waited patiently for my turn. BJ pushed Braylen in his walker into the living room where we were all sitting. Everyone fell out laughing because he was pushing poor Braylen fast as hell. BJ had finally started walking and his little butt was always into some shit. My nephews looked really cute in their custom-made Armani suits that were all white with silver hanks and vest to match Brook's.

"Stop!" BJ yelled when the makeup artist turned to pinch his little cheeks.

Again, we all fell out laughing. He couldn't talk for shit but his favorite words were mommy, da-da, stop, and shit. Looking on at the boys made me wonder what my child would look like. We had strong genes so I knew he would probably look like my brothers.

"You ready, baby?" the makeup artist called out to me.

I took my seat in her chair and let her beat my face.

After we were done, I went into the den and took another seat to wait patiently for Diane to get her makeup done so we could leave. I was so ready to go now because I was anxious about seeing Que. He loved Cash for more than one reason so I knew he wouldn't miss this wedding for the world. The last wedding date, we didn't make it because we had gotten shot, but I remember him being so pumped up about the ceremony.

TRAP GYRL 3

"What's wrong, sis?" Brooklyn asked, knocking me from my daze. He took a seat next to me and he too looked as if he had a lot on his mind.

I looked at him and sighed because I didn't want him to know the real, but knowing him, he would.

"Nothing, I'm fine." I smiled, but the look he gave me just let me know he had seen right through me.

"You miss him, don't you?" he asked, already knowing the answer.

I didn't even respond, I just nodded my head yes.

"I know you do, Bree. And, I also know how love could be. I'm not mad at you for how you feel, nor am I mad at Que. I'm pretty much over this shit. I just want our lives to go back to normal. You know, I never put you in our business, but once we kill this nigga, Mario, our lives will be back to normal."

"I'm pregnant!" I blurted out and began to weep.

Brook didn't say anything so I assumed he was stunned. When I looked at him, he wore a confused expression but remained quiet. I didn't mean to say it but Brook and I were so close, I knew he was the only one I could trust with the information. If Carter found out, he would die and take me with him.

"Damn, Bree." Brook stood to his feet and rubbed his hands down his face.

"I'm sorry." I cried harder.

Seeing me cry, his face softened and he sat back down next to me.

"There's nothing to be sorry about. Shit happens, ma. Look at my situation, I have two babies that are a few months apart, and them little dudes make life worth living for. It's not a bad thing and one hunnit, rather Que here or not, you know my nephew or niece gone be straight. I don't know if I ever told you this, Bree, but I'm so proud of you. You didn't follow in the footsteps of me and Carter. I mean, you got yo' head on straight, you smart, you got goals, and more important, you're the best person God has created. In all honesty, a baby is a blessing and you deserve it." He smiled and hugged me.

Just hearing this come from Brook made me light up like a kid at Christmas. Nobody in the world opinion mattered to me like his, and I was now thankful I decided to tell him.

Blaze & Tiny...

Barbie Scott
TRAP GYRL 3

I grabbed the two duffel bags I had equipped
with three MG3 machine guns, two AK-47, and five
9 millimeter handguns in each. I threw one bag to
Tiny and strapped the other over my shoulder. After
all the bullshit that went down at the last wedding, I
had to be all the way on point. Even though we
would be on the water and in the Bahamas, I still
didn't put shit past the Cartel. We had a shit load of
guards and snipers, but I felt like nobody has my
back like me. I needed my peoples safe, and
especially, my wife and kids.

After this wedding, Tiny and I decided she
would fall back from this street shit. She was about
to have my baby and I needed her clear. I promised
her that we would move next month into a seven-
bedroom mansion and her ass was happy as hell.
Just looking at her in the Naeem Khan beaded dress
made me admire her more. She was sexy as hell,
now thick in all the right places and she had a
beautiful pregnant glow.

The kids had left in the limo to meet with the
other kids because we didn't want them riding with
all these straps. All the kids were riding in their own
limo and Tiny's fourteen-year-old daughter would
be leading the pack.

Barbie Scott
TRAP GYRL 3

Walking out the door, I had a weird feeling, for some odd reason. I don't know if it was because of the last wedding or what, but something just wasn't right. When we made it outside the door, Tiny locked up the house and we made our way to the garage.

As soon as we stepped near the entrance, there was a swarm of police. I had a strap in my hand and so did Tiny because these were the guns that would be sitting on our laps as we drove to the yacht.

"Drop the weapon!" one of the officers yelled over the bull horn.

I looked over at Tiny who looked scared as hell and all I could do is shake my head. We had enough guns on us to send us away for the rest of our lives, and not to mention, why the fuck was they even here? I had laid so many people down and sold so much dope, it wasn't no telling why the fuck these crackers were here.

Tiny began to cry and that shit hurt a nigga heart.

"Drop the guns, now!" again, the officer yelled. It looked like the whole MPD was here to arrest.

Tiny slowly walked towards them. I called her name but she kept walking. They were yelling, stop right there, but out of fear, she was trying to surrender herself.

"Tiny, Nooo!" I yelled out again and she refused to stop.

"Stop right there or we will be forced to shoot," was the last thing I heard before they began firing shots into her tiny frame and stomach.

The last bullet to the head crushed every part of my soul. Her body instantly dropped and she fell on top of her stomach. She laid still and the way the blood seeped from her body, I knew she was indeed dead.

For the first time in my life, I cried like a bitch. I reached into my pocket and pulled out the rolled blunt I had, but making sure not to drop my gun. I pulled off my suit coat with ease and dropped it to the ground. Taking puffs off the blunt, I cried my eyes out. I eyed the officers as they watched me, closely. After the blunt was halfway gone, I dropped it to the ground. I clutched my gun in both hands and watched on as the officers told me, repeatedly, to drop my weapon. With so much hatred and force, I began blazing my gun, letting off every bullet I had. Some officers ducked for cover and some began to fire back.

Barbie Scott
TRAP GYRL 3

"Fuck the police!" I shouted as my body jerked forcefully from all the bullets I had taken to the chest. Before I knew it, I felt a burning sensation coming from my head. I dropped to the ground and I had no more fight in me.

But for Tiny, I didn't care. I went out like a Soulja with my girl.

Chapter XXX

Cash & Brooklyn Carter

The Wedding...

It was finally my wedding day and I was the happiest woman in the world. I wasn't nervous or scared of anything. I had a great feeling that everything would go smoothly and I held on to that fate. I wore an extravagant Valentino gown, and my hair and makeup were slayed. I had my makeup-artist and stylist on the yacht to touch me up upon arrival. Everybody was out on the deck, partying, while I chilled in my room waiting for the yacht to take off. The only reason we hadn't moved was because we were waiting for Blaze and Tiny to aboard the ship. I had just talked to them when the kids arrived in their limo and they said they were on the way. The Captain kept saying we would have to leave soon but I wasn't leaving without my best friends.

Brooklyn walked into the door and this was our first time seeing each other since I had been dressed. He watched me hungrily as if he wanted to strip me naked right there on the spot. The last wedding, we decided not to see each other until I walked down the altar, but this time, we were doing things a little different. We would chill on the boat, drinking champagne, and when we pulled up to the Bahamas, the pastor would be right there waiting. He would marry us, then everyone would board the yacht for the reception. The yacht would be taking everyone back to Miami, except immediate family because we were all staying to turn up in the Bahamas.

"You look beautiful, Mrs. Carter."

"Thank you, Mr. Carter," I blushed and reached out for his hand.

He kissed my neck, then each cheek, and hit me with his sexy ass smile. Looking into Brook's eyes, he looked like he was the happiest man alive. It made me think of the last time we were on the podium, he looked worried and stressed out; but not today. He looked confident and that shit made me feel great inside.

TRAP GYRL 3

"Bae, we gotta get the boat going. The pastor will be there waiting for us."

"But, bae, I don't wanna leave Blaze and Tiny."

"I know, ma. But they slacking and we gotta roll. Have you called them to see where they were at?"

"Yes, four times. Neither one is answering. I hope nothing is wrong." I began to think of the worst.

"Hell nah, ma. Blaze holding twenty-four guns, trust me, that nigga is straight," Brook said and eased my thoughts a bit.

This shit was like Deja Vu.

"I'ma send Kellz and a few more guards to get them, then they gone hop on the speed boat to catch up, ok?"

"Yes," I nodded my head up down.

"Today is your day, ma. After the last time, I don't want shit to ruin this day. Don't stress, baby, they gone be okay, okay?"

Again, I simply nodded.

He kissed my forehead and walked out, I assumed to tell the captain to take off.

I walked over to the mini-bar and took a shot of D'usse to calm my nerves. Once I finally talked to Blaze and Tiny, I would be just fine.

TRAP GYRL 3

Nino…

I hated to leave Blaze and Tiny because I knew
how much it meant to Cash for them to be here, but
we had to get to sailing because we were already
behind schedule. We had another yacht that was
much faster than the one we were on, so the two
would board that one along with Kellz and a few
guards.

Once the yacht started to sail, I was more
anxious to give Cash my last name. After all the
bullshit that went on with the last wedding, I was
going to make sure that this go around would be
joyful. Even though we didn't go all out this time on
decorations, the trip alone equaled to the same price
I spent the first time. Like I said before, for Cash, it
was well worth it.

Looking out at the crowd we had, it made a
nigga feel real good inside. All the kids were
running around, happily, Ms. Lopez and Esco were
intertwined in each other. Pedro and Rosa were
mingling within the crowd, but what stuck out was
my sister looking out into the ocean like she had a
lot on her mind. I knew she was tripping because
Que hadn't shown up and that shit made me feel bad

TRAP GYRL 3

inside. I hoped like hell he would come, not only for
Bree but at least to for Cash. I knew he thought we
were all mad at him but had he shown up, I was
going to have a heart to heart with him.

Lydia and the kids had shown up without
Bronx, and I guess he, as well, was in his feelings
still. He had not answered not one of my calls but
he hadn't changed his number so I know he got
every last message. It was crazy because I had
called his Brazilian chick a few times and every
time, she told me he was either sleep or had just
left. The day he had finally shown up to their home,
she had sent me a text, telling me he had finally
come. I told her to tell him to call me but I guess he
said fuck me and the entire family. Once the
wedding was done and we got back to Miami, I was
going to get my family settled in and hop on my
private jet to Brazil.

"Da-da," BJ walked over to me, taking steps
with ease. I couldn't help but laugh because he
looked like he struggled to get to me.

Once he reached me, I scooped him up in my
arms and turned around to face the water.
Everything was so fascinating to him because he
looked out into the ocean then the sky in awe. The
surrounding was so calming and the slight breeze

felt good across my face. Braylen was asleep inside the yacht with Cash and that was good because he was fussy over a tooth coming in.

Cash had emerged from inside and it was like she sent me into a trance. I watched her closely as she mingled with the crowd. When we locked eyes, we held each other's gaze, then she smiled, shyly. She looked so fucking beautiful in her wedding gown, that it was taking everything in me not to take her inside and tear that ass up. Just watching her from across the yacht had my dick rock hard. I turned back around to face the water so no one would notice the bulge in my pants. I tried to think of all types of shit but it seemed as if nothing was working.

"Look, papi, a dolphin," I told BJ, hoping he would look in the direction I was pointing.

The little nickname I had given him stuck to me because that's what Ms. Lopez called him, so everyone adopted the name and even me.

When he finally saw the dolphin, another one appeared and his eyes lit up.

"Hey, son, are you ready?" I turned around at the sound of Esco's voice.

"Hell yeah, Sco. I'm ready to give yo' baby girl my last name."

TRAP GYRL 3

We both laughed.

"You know, I remember the day you guys bumped heads in mi casa. I tried my hardest to keep Cash away from you. She asked me a million times who you were and I'd always tell her don't worry about it."

"Awe, that's fucked up."

Again, we laughed.

"It was like fate brought you two together because no matter how hard I tried, y'all still ended up together. You know I could say I'm happy for ju and mi hija. I don't think there's no man in the world that would make her happier then you have," he spoke, then lit his Cuban cigar. He took a hit then looked out into the water. "You made mistakes, Cash had made mistakes, but you guys learned from it. Nobody is perfect. When I started seeing Lopez, I was married and she was too. We never gave up on each other and deep inside, I knew one day we would be together. We've been taking things slow, but its times for us to move on, hell, we getting old," he said and took another hit of his cigar.

I didn't understand what he meant about moving forward because these two were inseparable since she had been out of prison. I guess he wanted marriage but I'm sure we would soon find out.

"Thank you, Sco. I really appreciate that, man," I said and gave him a manly hug.

When we turned around, Cash, and Ms. Lopez was walking up on us, smiling from ear to ear.

"Ju ass holes better not be talking shit about us," Ms. Lopez said in her broken English.

Esco and I started laughing while Cash and Ms. Lopez smirked to each other.

"Nah, moms, we were just talking about how much we love y'all two crazy ladies."

"I no loca. A little insane, but loca, no," Ms. Lopez said and laughed.

"Like mother like daughter." I shook my head, and again, we all burst out into laughter.

Ms. Lopez grabbed BJ from my arms and he began laughing. He wrapped his arms around her neck and buried his face into her neck.

"Mi, Papasito lindo." Ms. Lopez began talking her damn Spanish. She raised him into the air and shook him slightly, making him crack up laughing. "BJ, you take over the game for Abuelita. I getting too old, papi," she said, and BJ laughed as if he understood what she was saying.

I didn't know rather to laugh or what, because I somewhat believed Ms. Lopez was dead ass serious about what she said. I wanted BJ to become something in life, but in this game, you never know.

My father passed me and Bron the torch, but because I was the more level headed one, I ran it. Once I got old, BJ would be the next in command, except, I planned to get out the game before his next birthday. That was something else I wanted to holla at Cash about once we got back home. I was opening my restaurant in Cali, I had more money than I could count, so I would be leaving my empire to Kellz. However, who would be getting Ms. Lopez's?

Cash...

Just like Brook had said, the Pastor was on the island awaiting our arrival. He grabbed my hand and smiled, making me blush. I couldn't help it, I began to cry. Every tear that fell were happy tears but I was beyond happy; I was ecstatic.

Finally, I thought as we walked the plank to where the Pastor stood.

He stood with his head up high and his hands crossed over the front of him. The smile he gave me warmed my heart, and I was now more ready than before.

We walked up to the pastor and everyone crowded around us in a huge circle. Everyone was cheering us on and it only made me cry more.

"Stop crying, Mija, you're gonna ruin you makeup," my mother said and made everyone laugh.

Minister: Dearly Beloved, we are gathered here today to witness the union of,

Brooklyn Carter and Cash Lopez, in holy matrimony, which is an honorable

estate, that is not to be entered unadvisedly or lightly, but reverently and

soberly.

Into this estate, these two persons' present come now to be joined.

If anyone can show just cause why they may not be lawfully joined together, let them speak now or forever hold their peace.

That was all I had heard before I blacked out. I started thinking back to the day of our last wedding when Tiffany ran into the wedding to stop our marriage. Soon after, shots had ring out and it was like a damn massacre right there in the chapel. The

TRAP GYRL 3

horrific scene before my eyes was something like out of a movie. The many bodies I had witness fall to the ground was a memory that would forever be stuck with me. Not to mention, my best friend's death. Just the thought of Niya, made me cry harder. Everything the pastor was saying was a blur and I was stuck in a nightmare.

I began to think about Blaze and Tiny, who weren't there, and still didn't answer their phones. Something told me that shit wasn't right, but I tried my hardest to think positive. I said a silent prayer to myself and then the sound of Brooklyn's voice brought me back.

"Cash," he said my name, knocking me from my thoughts.

"Cash Lopez, do you take Brooklyn Carter Sr, to be your lawfully wedded husband?"

"I DO!" I shouted, making sure everyone had heard me.

"By the authority vested in me, I now pronounce you husband and wife. You may kiss your bride," the Pastor said and smiled between the two of us.

Brook grabbed my face in his hands and kissed my so passionately, it was like the first kiss we had ever shared. The crowd went wild and everyone began to throw rice at us. It was too funny because I had never seen not one person with any rice.

Once we were completely done, the pastor blessed us and we made our way back to the yacht. The second yacht pulled up to board our friends that were going back to Miami and my family and I were ready to continue our celebration.

Looking onto my family, I was trying my hardest not to let anything ruin my day, but it was hard. Blaze and Tiny were MIA, and Que hadn't shown up. I know I had said some fucked up things to him, but I was mad. At this very moment, I wished I could take it all back because I loved Que to death and I wished he had been here to enjoy this day with us. The moment I got back to Miami, I was going to call him and apologize, sincerely.

"Congratulations, Cash!" Nina, Nikki, Diane, and Breelah ran over and shouted.

We all hugged in a group right when Money walked up.

"Congrats, ma," Money said and hugged me tightly. He had Nina's ass beaming and that shit made me happy.

I looked at Breelah, who looked off into space, and I knew exactly what was on her mind. Just knowing my little sis was hurting, saddened me a little more. What really stuck out was the glow she had. I watched her closely and something was off about her.

Her ass is pregnant, I thought to myself.

Then focused my attention on BJ, who was now in the arms of Pedro. I loved the way BJ bonded with Pedro, he smiled, laughed, and held on tightly to Perdo's shirt. I walked over to the two and placed a big kiss on their cheeks. As soon as the yacht began to sail, that's when the yells and screams began. The sound of constant bottle popping was all that could be heard. The DJ began to play the song I had requested so I scanned the yacht for my husband. It was like an intuition because our eyes met, instantly. I began to mouth the words to the songs as he watched me with passion in his eyes.

Usually, when two people are together for a long-time, things seem to change.

It's been said nothing good lasts forever but this love gets better every day.

We get all excited inside every time that we get alone.

He still got love in his eyes, and I still got love in my soul.

Barbie Scott
TRAP GYRL 3

Still, feels like the first time we met that I kissed and I told you I love you,
We still run around like teenagers even though we're grown and married with kids,
and we still talk on the phone for hours when I'm away and he still writes letters and send me flowers every other day,
the question everybody asks is how we make it last
I tell them
I still
he still
we still...

Brook walked over to me and took me into his arms. Just the way he held me, made me feel like the luckiest woman alive. After today, we would go home as a married couple and nothing would ever tear us apart.

"Here you go, Mrs. Carter," the boat attendant handed me a glass of champagne.

"Thank you." I smiled, then grabbed the glass. I gulped it and grabbed the entire bottle from the porcelain tray and he chuckled, along with Brooklyn. I didn't care, this was my day and I was about to get fucked up. Brooklyn already had a

TRAP GYRL 3

bottle nestled in his hands so we took a swig together.

"Mrs. Carter, a nigga love you to death." Brooklyn looked me in the eyes. "I know I did some fucked up things in the past but I've right all my wrongs to make you happy. There's no woman in this world that could amount to you. This shit is till death, ma," Brooklyn said in a slurred tone.

I looked at him, I could tell everything he said was sincere. I was so caught up in the moment, I couldn't even respond. I kissed his soft lips before speaking, then…

BOOM!!!

I fell to the ground. My body seemed to be in such a pain that was indescribable. I don't know what happened, but the feeling I was having made me wish it was all a dream. Blood began to cover my entire wedding gown. I tried my hardest to look around the yacht, and the first thing I spotted was the two bottles that laid next to me that Brook and I had been drinking.

With much force, I began scanning the room. Brooklyn's body laid lifeless next to me, covered in blood. His legs were missing and the sight before me was a horrible one. I began to cry harder for Brook and the pain I endured myself. My eyes weakly scanned the entire boat, it was like everyone on the yacht was dead. My mother laid lifeless, my friends laid lifeless, and even my dad was dead. The top of the boat was on fire and it seemed to be growing wider. Braylen was back inside sleep off medicine because of his teeth, and that pained me more that I couldn't get up to try and save him.

My baby, I cried out, thinking about BJ. I didn't see him and Pedro anywhere.

Maybe it was best I didn't because I knew that would be a horrific sight to see. Feeling defeated, I was ready to give up. I couldn't imagine life without my family. My mom was all I had, I had just met my real father, and much worst I was only a mother for one year. I guess it was true, Karma came back around twice. I had done much in my lifetime, how could I not meet the bitch Karma herself. I had plenty bodies under my belt and I as well had deceived people in my lifetime. But the worst part of it all, is my friends and their children who were now dead because of my own demise. I never meant for innocent people to get hurt because of my lifestyle. For the first time in my life, I regret the life I lived. I knew that it couldn't be anyone but the Cartel that succeeded with such a stunt, and I also knew that a lot of this was behind Que and

Carter. But the truth of the matter is, The Cartel had it out for my mother many years ago. I closed my eyes because I knew this was the end for me.

Heavenly Father, I come to you to ask for forgiveness. Please forgive me for all the sins I had committed in my lifetime. Please protect BJ's little soul if he makes it from this horrible tragedy.

I prayed and drifted into a dark place. I took my last breath because I wanted to join my mother, father, and my husband. There was nothing left on this earth for me to live for, so I simply gave up. *Sigh.*

The end...

TRAP GYRL 3

Epilogue

Que...

"Hello?" This nigga answered on what seemed like the hundredth ring.

"Tell me something good, Negro."

"It's done!" was all I said into the phone and quickly disconnected.

I know what y'all are thinking, *Que ain't shit*. But, y'all been knowing that so why act surprised now. I knew how much everyone loved Cash, hell, I loved her too. But, in this game, its kill or be killed; straight up. Since everyone was mad at me, anyway, and the Cartel was paying me ten million, I did what I had to do or I'd be a dead man myself. No, I wasn't about to work for them niggas but I would be taking over Ms. Lopez's empire and be the man I'd been before.

I knew that one day, me having Cash's phone tracked would eventually pay off, and guess what? Today was the day. I tracked her phone in the middle of the ocean, and boom, I blew that

muthafucka up. Everybody was on the ship dead
and even the love of my life, Breelah. Y'all know
ya boy Quintin, pussy comes a dime a dozen. No
lie, I would miss baby girl but after that night she
chose her brother over me, told me I couldn't trust
her ass. I hated to do Ms. Lopez like that but she
had to go as well. I wanted her empire but I would
make sure to keep her memory alive.

When the boat blew up, I could have sworn I
saw Pedro and BJ fall into the water. But, with that,
Big Ivan, better known as Tsar Bomba, the entire
combined firepower expended in WWII, I knew
everybody was dead. And, even if they had
survived, they wouldn't last too long in 36,000 feet
of water.

Once I made it back to my car, I jumped on I-
95, headed to me Gabriela's hotel room so we could
head back to Brazil. Yeah, you heard right. I had
been smashing that thick ass Brazilian bitch since
Carter first brought her to the states. I caught that
ass the day of Nina's baby shower the moment Bree
had turned her back and slid her my number. All
them lonely nights in her hotel room, well, let's not
say lonely because every chance I got I was fucking
her brains out. I got in so good with the hoe, I had
her kill Carter and even get Keisha and Qui a house

Barbie Scott
TRAP GYRL 3

around the corner from us in her name. I'm now living in Carter's mansion, and with my BM and child close by, was all I needed in this life. I got enough money to last a lifetime. I'm talking so much money, I could live another hundred years and even my daughter would be straight once I died. Not to mention, the dough I'm bout to collect from Mario.

Life has just gotten better.

Barbie Scott
TRAP GYRL 3

*I would like to dedicate this novel to my best
friend, forever.*

"Claude Thomas" a.k.a. "Outlaw Smokey."

*I love you to death, BFF, and through every
journey, good times and even bad, you've been by
my side. You never judged me and you didn't
throw stones when I was down. We've supported
each other and had each other's back when the
world gave us their ass to kiss. I'm dreading the
day you'll return to the streets and complete my
life.*

*PS. You're like the only missing piece to the
puzzle. Once again, I love you, foo.
FREE YOU, FAST! #BottomsUp #230 #Whoop*

Made in the USA
Lexington, KY
26 November 2019